IV

THE STALKING HORSE

Previous books by the same author:

An Evil Hour
A Perfect Match

JILL McGOWN
THE STALKING HORSE

ST. MARTIN'S PRESS
NEW YORK

Library of Congress Cataloging-in-Publication Data

McGown, Jill.
      The stalking horse.

      "A Thomas Dunne book."
      I. Title.
PS3563.C365S7   1988   813'.54   88-15834
ISBN 0-312-02291-3

First published in Great Britain by Macmillan London Limited.

First U.S. Edition

10 9 8 7 6 5 4 3 2 1

According to the *Shorter Oxford English Dictionary*, a stalking horse is a person whose participation in a proceeding is made use of to prevent its real design from being suspected.

One

Bill Holt swung the case down from the luggage rack as the familiar landmarks, still there, came into view. Home. It didn't feel like coming home. No one knew he was coming, and if they had known, no one would have been there to meet him.

He watched as other people gathered their belongings. The driver spoke to them again, telling them not to forget anything. The others didn't find it odd that the train driver spoke to them, like an airline pilot. They didn't find it odd that they could get off the train and go where they pleased. They took their liberty for granted.

Holt didn't. His had been snatched from him, almost sixteen years ago. This was the same train, near as damn it, as the one he'd been on that day.

He stood up and stretched as the tyre depot came into his field of vision. He liked his Friday mornings in London. Maybe he should talk to Bob about a transfer. He'd been thinking about it for some time. But he knew that it wasn't really a change of job to which he'd been giving so much thought. He'd been thinking about ending his marriage, and a transfer to London was one way out. He could talk to Bob, unofficially. Just to see if there was a possibility of a transfer.

A few others moved along the swaying corridors with him. He caught sight of Jeff Spencer coming the other way, and hung back, because he didn't really want to have to make polite conversation.

Thomas Jefferson Spencer was, not surprisingly, an American – mid-thirties, handsome, bright – he looked a little like an advertisement for something. He was trying to interest Greystone in some idea of his, and Bob Bryant and Ralph were taking him very seriously. But right now, Holt thought, he looked a

1

little care-worn for a man about to spend the weekend with his bride-to-be.

The train squealed to a halt, and Holt made his way to the doors.

Holt found himself on one of the new platforms – new to him, though clearly familiar to the other passengers. They had been under construction when he had last been in the station.

Doors slammed, and his train drew away. Holt looked at the lines, glinting in the sun, snaking on into the distance, and watched the train as it rattled its way into the Midlands. He sat down, barely aware of the slight drizzle that was flecking the new clothes he'd bought that morning in London.

'What were you looking for?' the assistant had asked.

'Anything,' he'd said. 'Casual, fashionable. Not blue, and not denim.'

The boy had accepted the provisos without comment. And then he'd kitted him out with fawn slacks, a brown shirt, and a baggy jacket that seemed too large for him, but the boy had said that that was how they were wearing them. And Holt had gone over to the door, and looked out at the people who were passing. 'So they are,' he'd said.

'Have you been away?' the boy had asked, and Holt had said yes. And then he had put his other clothes into the bag, and taken them to an Oxfam shop.

The boy's hair had been short and slicked back. But Holt had looked at the people that he'd passed, and men of his age – almost forty-five, my God, he'd been a month short of his twenty-ninth birthday when it happened – still wore theirs the way it came. Shorter than his, perhaps, he had thought. So he had gone into a barber's.

He looked across the lines to the old platforms. The telephone box was in the same place, but it had changed too, with large panels of glass where there had been little panes. If only he could recall his time, if only he could telephone for a taxi instead of what he did do.

He put the package down on the ledge, and searched his pockets for a shilling, tipping the cardboard box up as he did so. He caught it, his heart in his mouth, for in the box was the specially ordered glassware that Wendy was giving Mrs Warwick as a wedding present. Somehow, it was Mrs Warwick's wedding, and Wendy's present. The men didn't seem to have much to do with it. He balanced the box more securely, and found the coin.

He could ring Wendy, see if she was back from Leicester yet, but he wouldn't. Trust there to be no taxis in the station when he needed one; he couldn't remember any taxi numbers, and the directory was under the box. He sighed, made to slide the book out, then changed his mind. He'd ring Bob Bryant, see if he fancied a drink.

He dialled the private number that rang on Bryant's desk, the chairman's perk. Ralph Grey had finally retired from office, though not from the board, in April. Now Bryant was officially running the company, which he had been doing for years anyway. He persuaded the shilling to go in just before the pips ran out.

'Hello?'

Holt frowned. That was Alison's voice. Had he dialled their home number by mistake? 'Alison?' he said.

'Yes,' she said, laughing a little. 'Hello, Bill.'

'What are you doing there?' he asked.

'I came in to see Cassie about something,' she said. 'Then I came in here, and the phone rang. Bob's not in the office – can I leave him a message?'

'Oh, no thanks. I just thought he might fancy a drink.'

'Not tonight,' she said. 'They're all working late tonight, I'm told. I'm surprised Bob comes home at all, frankly.'

'Is the board meeting still going on?' he asked, glancing at his watch. It was five fifteen.

'No, but he's still in there,' she said. 'Do you want me to get him?'

'Oh, no. No. I was just cadging a lift, really. Wendy's got the car.'

'Where are you?' she asked. 'At the station?'

'Yes, but —'

'I'll come and get you, if you like.'

3

'No,' he said. 'It's too much trouble — I'll get a taxi.'

'It would be no trouble,' she said. 'And . . . well, I'd like to see you. Talk to you. I'll explain when I get there. I'll be there in ten minutes. All right?'

'Sure,' said Holt, a little puzzled, and hung up.

Cigarettes. He needed cigarettes.

Cigarettes. He could go down the underpass, over to the kiosk, and buy cigarettes. All those cigarettes.

The echoes in the tunnel made him shiver, reviving memories of the remand prison. That had been the worst; the initial heart-stopping shock of hearing locks turn.

He emerged from the underpass, and went into the kiosk.

'Tea,' he said, and he thought she must have made a mistake when she said how much she wanted.

'I just want tea,' he said.

'Yes,' she said.

Christ.

He sat down with his cup, and looked out at the station. A bell rang, three times. A station announcement was made, and it was piped right into the kiosk. Suddenly, as if it had just been a joke, the rain stopped, and it was sunny and warm again, as it had been all day.

After he'd been sentenced — life imprisonment, the judge had said, and he couldn't take it in — after he'd been sentenced, he had been in one or two prisons before they had almost brought him home, for Gartree wasn't far from here. The train he had just been on would be pulling into Leicester any minute now. Gartree. He was Category A, a danger to the public. A lifer.

And that's what it means, he had been told. You are being released on licence. You can be recalled, if the circumstances warrant it, at any time, for the rest of your life. If you show any homicidal tendencies.

The last couple of years had been at an open prison, and he had been able to work outside. On the land sometimes, and in work parties, on derelict buildings, pulling them down or patching them up. He had lost his prison pallor. On the outside. But there was a cold greyness on the inside that he couldn't lose.

4

He'd kept healthy. He'd grown leaner, and fitter, and stronger. His hair was still dark, and still there. He was older, but he hadn't changed much, not to look at. But those who really knew Bill Holt before he went in would see a change; a hardening of the man, a more defiant set to his jaw, a colder look in his eye. He had learned first how to defend himself, and then how to put others on the defensive. How to hurt them. It was easy to hurt people. Emotionally, physically — it didn't much matter which. The two were never far apart. Use the crushing mechanism on one, and you affect the other.

To begin with, he had wasted time by continuing to protest his innocence. He had twice tried to appeal against the conviction, and been turned down. He had read legal books and precedents, and tried to do it himself when the legal profession said they'd done all they could. But no one had believed him. No one had listened. And they weren't about to start listening just because he was sitting on the roof shouting himself hoarse at reporters who couldn't hear him. All he got out of that was solitary confinement.

And one night, lying alone in a cell, he had realised that it was a losing battle. He had cried.

He pushed away his empty cup, and left the kiosk.

'Thanks,' he said, putting the cigarettes in his pocket, and picking the box up from the counter.

He wondered what Alison wanted to talk to him about. She'd be here any minute, he realised, looking at the clock, and left the kiosk just as Spencer came in. Spencer was a super-keen amateur photographer, and he always looked like a tourist, with his ever-present camera-case. One of his hobbies was turning the tables on London cabbies.

'Bill — I thought that was you on the train.'

'Nice to see you again,' said Holt. 'Sorry, I can't stop, someone's meeting me.'

'Maybe I'll see you tomorrow,' said Spencer, 'at Thelma's get-together?'

Damn. He'd forgotten about that. 'Of course,' he said, smiling.

Thelma Warwick was almost ten years older than Spencer, and

the widow of one of Greystone's major shareholders. Her eldest son had been killed in a hit-and-run accident a few months before, and it was this, Holt fancied, which had cemented the relationship, because Jeff Spencer had been on hand to see her through her grief. A quiet wedding, it had been agreed by the family, was what Roger would have wanted.

Spencer held open the door for him, as he negotiated the box through the crush. 'See you,' he said.

He was being unfair to Jeff, really, he supposed. He was in business himself, and obviously substantial enough for Greystone to be listening seriously to his proposition. But while he may not actively have been hunting a fortune, Thelma did, fortuitously, provide one.

It was that rarity: a warm, sunny, blue-skied July day. Holt wanted, for a moment, to drop the precious glassware and leap on the first train going anywhere. But he didn't, and he smiled as he saw Alison hurrying towards him. She looked more beautiful than ever, he thought, as she came up to him and kissed him on the cheek.

'The car's miles away,' she said.

They were enlarging the station, which was battling against the tide, and had more users than it could accommodate. He saw Spencer again, looking round for the hire car that always awaited him at the station, and was illogically pleased that Alison was there. It did your reputation no harm to have a beautiful woman coming to meet you.

They walked to the car where, after some discussion as to where it would be safest, he put the wedding present in the boot.

It was after he had been transferred to Gartree that he had come to a decision. If he was going to be a prisoner, then he was going to get bloody good at it. He wasn't going to spend years and years of his life running from the bully-boys on either side of the bars. He would get hard and strong and fast. And they would jump when he said jump, because he had a brain to back up his brawn, unlike most of them. And only once did his wit desert him long enough to get caught. It had cost him more solitary, and it had

6

left him with a scar on his upper arm, but it had been worth it.

His first two requests for parole were refused, but now, third time lucky, he was out. But no coming-out party for him. He'd lost his wife, his friends, and his youth. But he was back now. And on his thirtieth birthday he had become a shareholder in Greystone. Grandfather Stone had had the good sense to die the Christmas before it all happened, or he might even have been cheated out of that.

He had had sixteen years to think about this moment, plan for it, look forward to it. It had kept him going during prison officers' industrial disputes, when he had been shut up for twenty-three hours out of the twenty-four, and through the winter nights, when it seemed that the sun would never shine again. It had taken the place of sexual fantasy, of dreams, of hope. One thing had kept him sane, one thing had lent him a little warmth and colour. His plan.

Methodically, carefully, he was going to find out who had murdered Alison and that detective. And when he did, he was going to kill whoever it was.

It was as simple, and as beautiful, as that.

The prison governor had been doubtful about his going back home, but he'd agreed to support him. 'An hotel?' he'd said. 'Well, all right. That seems like a good idea. Until you know what you want to do.' And he'd warned him that he might get a bad reception. And no doubt phoned the police to warn them, too.

He had to report to a probation officer, of all things. 'Once a week to start with,' they'd said. 'Until we know how you're settling back into the community.'

And he'd nodded, and listened, his sharp grey eyes reading upside down what was on the governor's desk.

'*As far as we can ever be sure of these things,*' it had read, '*Holt's rehabilitation seems to have been a success. I hope he will make a go of returning to his community, if they allow him to.*'

He had thanked the governor for his advice.

The cars in the station car park didn't look too different − a lot of black where there used to be chrome, and prices that he thought were what you paid for semi-detached houses – but not really much different. He walked up the hill from the station; it was a one-way road now.

'So,' he said, as they drove up Station Road. 'What's the mystery?'

'What mystery?' she asked.

She was checking her rear-view mirror every now and then, like a pupil trying to impress the driving examiner. Holt glanced back, but there was nothing unusual about the tail-back of traffic.

'Whatever it is you want to talk to me about,' he said.

'It's a bit . . .' She didn't finish the sentence. 'Will you come to the house?' she asked. 'I'd like you to see something.'

Holt frowned. He'd known Alison all his life; there wasn't a time when he hadn't known her. She'd never found it difficult to talk to him before. 'What's wrong?' he asked.

'Nothing,' she said. 'Will you?'

'Of course.'

She seemed edgy. Almost as though she were nervous of him.

'Something's wrong,' he said.

Alison was Ralph Grey's daughter; the Greys and the Stones had founded Greystone Office Equipment together, and in the early days, had practically lived together. He, Alison, and his cousin Cassie had grown up together, and Alison had never felt ill at ease with him in her life.

'Come on,' he said. 'You'd better tell me.'

'I'm in trouble,' she said. 'But let's leave it until we get to the house.'

She always called it the house. Never home. Still, they hadn't been there very long.

'Why were you inviting Bob for a drink?' she asked.

'Is it that unusual?'

'It is a bit,' she said. 'He doesn't know how to have time off. He only understands business drinks.'

Holt smiled. Well, it would have been a business drink, of a sort. He'd wanted to sound him out about London. And he wondered, not for the first time, why Alison had married Bob

Bryant, seventeen years older than her, and a company man from the roots of his hair to his toes. Perhaps that was the problem, he thought. He'd soon find out.

He walked slowly, noting every change, until he got to where High Street used to be. Still was, according to the sign. But it had changed so much that he didn't really know where he was going. The George must still be there, or they would have told him. He pressed his lips together in annoyance. 'They' no longer ran his life. They no longer fed and clothed and housed him. They no longer told him what to do and when to do it, and how to do it. They couldn't take away his privileges or his identity any more.

But they could make him report to a probation officer, they could insist on knowing where he was living, and they could recall him at any time if he showed homicidal tendencies.

In London that morning, he had called in at his solicitor's office before he had done anything else. He had picked up a case full of papers, papers which he'd told them he would want. A transcript of the trial, every piece of evidence, every scrap of paper, everything they had written or that anyone else had written about him, or Alison, or Allsopp. All he knew about Allsopp was the police description of him; six foot two, medium build, brown hair. Thirty-four. He didn't even know what he had looked like, and he was supposed to have murdered the man.

And personal things — cheque book, ready cash — things he had told his solicitor to have ready for him. His driving licence — it was just a green piece of paper in a plastic folder. It expired in the year two thousand and eleven. He'd have to make a note to remember to renew it. He smiled at his own joke, which hadn't been voiced, for who had been there to listen for the last sixteen years?

'Are you sure about going home, Bill?' his solicitor had asked.

'Yes.' He had stowed the personal stuff away in various pockets.

'You could always change your mind.'

'No, I couldn't. I've said that's where I'm going. If I go anywhere else they'll have me back in Gartree before I can blink.'

'No, they won't, and you know it,' he'd said crossly. 'I'll sort it all out.'

'I'm going home.'

'But have you thought about it?' he'd asked.

Thought about it, breathed it, lived it, eaten it.

'Yes,' he'd said.

'They aren't going to put out the welcome mat – it's a small town.' He had sighed, an exasperated sigh. 'Have you told them you're coming?'

Holt's features had frozen. 'No,' he had said slowly, and he had leant on the desk, his face close to the other man's. 'And if you have,' he had said quietly, 'you will be very sorry that you did.'

He had seen the fear. Just a few words, and a bit of body language, and you could produce fear.

'I haven't,' he'd said, so obviously relieved that it had to be the truth.

'Good.' And he had held the position for a moment, before relaxing and straightening up.

The solicitor had shuffled some papers about his desk then. 'I'm only thinking of you, Bill,' he'd said.

'Thank you.' He had walked to the door.

Once the space between them had grown, the solicitor's nerve had returned. 'If you cause any trouble, they will have you back in Gartree,' he'd said.

'No trouble,' Holt had said. 'You have my word.'

He needed a car. He took one of the side roads off what used to be High Street. There used to be a car showroom there, from which Spencer had rented his cars, once he'd got rid of the American job he had called the gas-guzzler. Petrol cost too much in this country, he had said. Holt wondered what he thought of it now.

It was there. New plate glass, and a new office.

'Could I see your licence please?' she asked.

He gave her the licence.

'Thank you. Could you wait a moment, Mr Holt?'

Mr Holt. It hit him like a truck. No one had called him Mr

10

Holt, not for fifteen years. They had called him Mr Holt in court.

'Did you ask her why she had done such a thing?'

He tried to stand up, and answer the question directly, as he'd been advised to. But his head hung down. 'No. I didn't speak.'

The prosecution counsel raised his eyebrows, and looked at the jury. Holt hadn't looked at them once since he'd started giving evidence. He'd watched them when Bryant gave evidence. And the taxi driver. And the police inspector. They looked as though they were listening, but how could you tell? They might be thinking what to have for supper, or wondering what won the two thirty. And if they were listening, what were they hearing? Evidence piling up against him.

'Did she speak?'

'She said she was sorry.'

'I repeat. What did you do?'

'I got dressed and left.'

'Got dressed, and left,' he repeated, glancing at the jury again, in the way he had, of sharing a joke with them. 'Got dressed, and left. Weren't you angry, Mr Holt?'

'Shocked.'

'Shocked. And, surely, angry? She had just put in jeopardy your marriage, and your job. She had certainly wrecked a friend-ship. She had betrayed you, Mr Holt. And I think you were angry. I think you were very angry.'

'I suppose so,' he said. But he hadn't been. Not really. He had been too shocked to be angry, too stunned by what she had done.

'And what did she do, while you were getting dressed, and leaving?'

Again, the sly look at the jury. Holt looked at them too, now. One of them was smirking, as if he were watching some sort of *risqué* comedy. 'Nothing,' he said, helplessly. 'She just . . . ' He moved his shoulders in a slight shrug. 'Nothing. She didn't do anything.'

'I think she got up, put on her bath-robe, and went down-stairs,' he said. 'And that you followed her.'

'No. She didn't get up. I just got dressed and left.'

11

'You knocked her unconscious, and you strangled her, with the tie of her bath-robe. That's what you did, isn't it, Mr Holt?'

'No,' he said, his voice agonised. 'No, no.'

'All right, Mr Holt. We'll follow your version of events. You got dressed and left. And when Mrs Bryant was shortly afterwards found dead, the police began a hunt for the man with whom she had had sexual relations prior to her death. That was you, Mr Holt. Why didn't you come forward?'

'Because . . . ' Why the hell did he suppose? Because at first they had held Bob for hours, then let him go. And then they were looking for him — *him*, thinking he had done it. Because it hadn't been him, and he didn't understand about the private detective. Because he was confused, and bewildered and frightened. 'I was frightened,' he said.

'Of what, Mr Holt? You had just got dressed and left, hadn't you?'

Yes. Yes. But everything had happened so quickly.

'When the police questioned you about your property being found in the boot of Mrs Bryant's car, you told a pack of lies, didn't you?'

'Yes.'

'And it wasn't until you were questioned in respect of Mr Allsopp's death that anything approaching the truth began to emerge.'

'No — it wasn't quite like that — I . . . I told the truth. It is the truth. This time.'

'This time? I put it to you that it is still a pack of lies. That you beat and strangled Mrs Bryant, and that when Mr Allsopp contacted you, saying that he was investigating Mrs Bryant's death, you panicked. You thought that he was the one Mrs Bryant had thought was watching her; that he had seen you at Mrs Bryant's house. I put it to you that you went to Mr Allsopp's caravan with the express intention of killing him, and that that is what you did.'

'No.' His voice was weak now.

'Do you deny having been in Allsopp's caravan on the afternoon of his death?'

12

Holt shook his head.

'Please answer aloud, Mr Holt,' said the judge.

Holt looked across at him. It was all right for him, sitting there in his silly clothes. 'No,' he said.

'Let me get this straight, Mr Holt,' said the prosecuting counsel. 'You are asking this court to believe that you just happened to be in Mrs Bryant's house immediately prior to her death, and in Mr Allsopp's caravan immediately post his?'

'Yes,' he said.

The car wasn't bad. And he could drive it easily enough. But the roads were incomprehensible. It was all one-way traffic and cobblestones in the middle of what used to be perfectly good streets. And traffic lights, my God, the traffic lights.

He hadn't checked in at the hotel. He had meant to, but his dream wouldn't be denied, not even for that. He'd do it later. Because today was Friday. It was the last Friday in June, and if he knew Bob Bryant, that was something that wouldn't have changed in sixteen years. The Greystone Office Equipment board meeting would still be held on the last Friday of the month, and Bill Holt was going to attend.

Because now he was out. And he was back.

'. . . and a man like you, who does not hesitate to kill whoever crosses him or threatens his security, must be kept away from the community for a very long time. You kill easily, without compunction, without remorse. I must therefore sentence you to life imprisonment, with a recommendation that you serve not less than fifteen years in prison . . .'

The judge's words rang in his ears as he drove. Fifteen years. He'd served his fifteen years and then some, on top of the months in custody before the trial. But now he was out.

He was out, he was back, and he was dangerous.

13

Two

Holt drove towards Greystone's head office, ostentatiously built with grey facing stone in the late sixties, even before it had mushroomed into the concern it was now. Not in London, which would have been more sensible, and where its executives had had to spend half their lives anyway. Not in Birmingham, or even Leicester, where it would have seemed more at home. But here, Ralph Grey had insisted. Here, where his roots were. And out of town, right on the edge of the countryside. He probably wouldn't get planning permission these days.

The firm was an amalgamation of Grey's Office Machines and Stone (Wireless) Ltd in the mid-thirties, before the war. Ralph Grey was very young and forward-looking; Arnold Stone was much older, much more forward-looking, and wonderfully eccentric. Together, they had become Greystone Office Equipment, producing everything from paper clips to internal telephone systems. And, late in 1969, along had come Thomas Jefferson Spencer, fresh-faced and youthful, full of American confidence, to tell them that the coming thing was microelectronics. It had taken him the best part of a year, but he had convinced them, and in the sixteen years that Holt had spent behind bars, Greystone had grown out of all recognition. Holt's bank balance had grown with it; he was a rich man.

Before the outbreak of war, Arnold Stone had purchased a huge folly of a building which had housed the headquarters of the firm, and both families. When Holt's mother married, the couple had simply moved in to a set of rooms. In due course, Ralph's wife and Holt's mother had produced babies within months of one another, and thus he had grown up with Alison. In the late fifties, the firm had grown, pushing the living quarters out, and they had acquired more conventional abodes. In the sixties, the head office was built, and the old house was demolished to accommodate a dual carriageway.

Ralph had marked down Holt as Alison's future husband, and he had been quite happy with the prospect. But the relationship, such as it was, had drifted, and they had grown merely friendly by the time they were twenty. There had never been anything definite, and he had met Wendy, and begun to wonder if marrying Alison was really what he wanted — not that marriage to anyone was top of his list of priorities. But Alison had pre-empted any statement he might have made concerning their future by suddenly announcing that she was to marry Bob Bryant, then Greystone's administration manager. Holt had been surprised, and a little hurt. Thirty-seven and divorced, Bryant was hardly the mate Ralph would have chosen for Alison, but he had given his permission readily enough. At least Bryant was highly suitable as far as the company was concerned. Holt had married Wendy when he was twenty-one, and his motives for doing so were unclear, even to him.

He was older now, and wiser. He parked the car in the car park under the Greystone building which stood on ugly stilts above him.

'I'm sorry,' Bryant's secretary said. 'It's board day – he won't be available until after five.'

'I'll just say hello,' Holt said.

'If you can give me your name . . .'

Holt winked, and opened the connecting door to Bryant's office, which was empty. He closed the door as the girl came scuttling after him, and strode to the board room.

He opened the door, and they looked up, like a class photograph. They were all there. Every one of them.

Bob Bryant, thin, nervy as ever. You could practically hear the ulcers growing. He was over sixty now, Holt realised, as Bryant took his spectacles off and frowned a little. At first he looked surprised by the interruption, then horrified when he recognised Holt.

Jeff Spencer, more handsome than ever in early middle age. He was still married to Thelma, despite all the mutterings at the time of how it wouldn't last. They gave smart dinner parties; Holt didn't suppose that he'd find himself on the guest list.

And Wendy. A little plumper than when he'd last seen her,

which hadn't been so long ago. She had done well out of the inevitable divorce. She had arrived at Greystone as a trainee accountant, and had stayed with the firm after they married, moving up the ladder as quickly as nepotism would allow. And when the dust on the trial and the divorce had settled, she had told him that Charles Cartwright had proposed her as a board member. He had thought she was mad, given the circumstances. And even without that, he couldn't see it happening. Ralph had had to swallow one woman on the board; he'd never go for two. But he had, despite everything.

At least they had stuck by Wendy, he thought, with grudging appreciation. But seeking election to the board still seemed an odd move for Wendy to have made, all the same. She had married again; perhaps he had been pulling her strings. Despite the divorce, despite her re-marriage, he had seen Wendy regularly, and she had kept him up to date with Greystone and its directors' doings.

Charles Cartwright. Smooth, well-educated Charles, his sand-coloured hair immaculately cut and styled as ever. Not a whizz-kid any more, but a successful man in his early fifties. He had been the youngest ever supervisor, section head, department head, you name it. At thirty-five, he had been the youngest board member, until Cassie came along. And he had been strongly tipped to become the youngest-ever chief executive, but Bryant had kept the job himself when he became chairman, and he had never relinquished it.

And Cassie. Cassie Stone, Holt's cousin, had come into her slice of Greystone on the death of their grandfather, having turned thirty that year. She had been free to take her seat on the board, unlike Holt. Cassie was blonde, and good looking in a tousled, untidy way. She hadn't changed all that much. None of them had. A little bit older, a little bit more what they had been. Balder, plumper, smoother.

'I'm out,' he said.

Bryant looked at the others before he spoke. 'I didn't think you would have the gall,' he said.

'Some of this company's mine,' Holt said steadily.

'That does not give you the right to come in here.'

Holt raised his eyebrows, and slammed the door shut in the face of Bryant's hovering secretary.

Spencer stood up. 'Shall I help him on his way?' he asked. The accent wasn't so noticeably American now, but what there was was still unmistakably Brooklyn. Spencer obviously fancied himself in a rumpus.

Holt took a step towards him. Spencer wasn't a tall man, and Holt stood close to him to accentuate his advantage. 'Sit down,' he said, looking into Spencer's blue eyes.

But he didn't see fear this time. He saw another look he knew. The look of someone assessing him, evaluating him, and deciding that it wasn't worth the risk. A street-fighter's look. Spencer shrugged, and sat down.

'I just want to ask for your help with something,' Holt said mildly, and took a chair from the ones lining the wall. He straddled it, leaning his arms on the back. 'All of you.'

'You expect our *help*?' Cassie said, and Holt's eyes flicked over to her. 'Go to hell,' she said.

'I've been,' said Holt. 'I don't recommend it. You see,' he went on, his eyes on each of them in turn, 'I didn't kill Alison. Or your private detective,' he said to Bryant. He looked round the table. 'One of you did.'

There was a general shuffling, a kind of flurry of movement, when he had spoken the words. A sort of communal turning away in embarrassed disbelief. One of them was faking it, and he was going to find out which.

'This is ridiculous,' Charles said, his fair skin reddening. 'This is some sort of sick game.'

Holt glanced at him; he stared malevolently back.

'So, let's see which of you doesn't want to help me.'

'No one wants to help you,' Charles said.

'Come on, Charles,' said Holt. 'I've been in prison for sixteen years. Sixteen years; think about it. I didn't kill Alison. And if you didn't, then you've nothing to lose by helping me. The only one who has anything to lose . . .' He finished the sentence with a shrug. 'What about you, Wendy? You promised to love,

17

honour and obey me once. Yes she did, Cassie, she promised to obey.'

Cassie didn't react.

'How?' Wendy asked. 'I couldn't help before, how can I help now?'

'Just answer any questions I ask you,' he said. 'That's all. I don't know what the questions will be yet. And I don't know when I'll be asking them. Will you do that for me?'

'It was a long time ago, Bill,' she said. 'I don't know if I'll remember.'

'Odd. I remember it as if it was yesterday.' He turned to Bryant. 'How can it hurt?' he asked.

'I gave my evidence at the trial,' Bryant said, his voice hostile.

'So you'll have no objections to my asking you to give it again?'

'I have the strongest possible objection to your being here at all.'

Holt nodded, and turned quickly. 'Charles. What about you?'

'I think this is some sort of lunatic idea that you thought up in prison, and I'm having nothing to do with it.' He stood up. 'And if you're going to stay here, I'm leaving.' He strode across the room, and banged the door behind him as he left.

'Jeff,' Holt said.

'I don't see how I can help you,' Spencer said, without animosity. 'I wasn't involved. How can I help?'

'I don't know. But if you can, will you?'

'I just don't see how. I mean, I wasn't even with the firm officially. I was still in London, if you remember. I'd never even met Alison.'

'No,' Holt said. 'But you'd seen her.' This was his first real attempt to get to grips with it. He watched Spencer carefully.

'Had I?' he asked, frowning.

'That evening. The very evening that she died.'

Spencer shook his head, still apparently puzzled.

'Alison picked me up at the station. And you were just behind us.'

Spencer's face cleared. 'Why yes, I remember seeing you with a girl. I just caught a glimpse, of course —'

18

'And in sixteen years it never occurred to you that that was Alison you saw?' Holt asked, interrupting him.

Spencer's blue eyes didn't blink. 'No,' he said.

Holt dropped it. 'Cassie?' he said. 'How about you?'

She nodded. 'I'll help you,' she said. 'If I can.'

Holt couldn't disguise his surprise. 'Just like that? No provisos, no disclaimers?'

She looked at him for a long time. 'I was certain that you had killed her,' she said. 'And they could have sliced you up into pieces for all I cared.'

'And now?'

'I can't believe you'd do this. Not after all this time. Not without a good reason.'

'One down, four to go,' he said.

Wendy cleared her throat. 'Well you know I'll help if I can,' she said. 'I've never thought you had anything to do with it.'

Holt nodded. 'Spencer?'

'Look, like I said. I don't see how I can help. And I think you'll only upset people by raking it all up again. I don't think it's fair on Bob.'

'Oh?' said Holt, his eyes amused. 'Are you and Bob big mates now? I seem to recall your saying that marrying the boss's daughter appeared to have been his most significant achievement.'

Bryant looked down at the minutes which lay abandoned in front of him, but Spencer wasn't at all put out.

'That was before,' he said. 'Before I knew anyone. I was wrong. I often am.' He smiled. 'But I don't know if you're on the level,' he said.

'Same here,' Holt replied.

'Maybe,' Spencer said thoughtfully. 'Maybe. Yes, I'll help. If I can.'

'Bob?' Holt said.

'You were tried,' said Bryant, barely audibly. 'And found guilty. Of murdering my *wife*. What sort of help do you expect from me?' He looked up. 'How could it have been anyone else? Who else could have done it? Why would anyone else have killed Allsopp?'

19

Holt realised that he hadn't bought cigarettes after all, and took one from Spencer's packet. Spencer flicked his lighter, and Holt inhaled deeply before he spoke.

'I've been locked up,' he said, 'for a long, long time. For something I didn't do. If I can convince you that someone else could have done it, will you help me then?'

Bryant looked at the other three, and didn't speak.

'I'd like to move that this board meeting be adjourned,' Holt said. 'All those in favour?'

They all looked a little embarrassed, and Spencer stood up. 'OK, Bob?' he asked.

Bryant nodded, and the others filed out of the room.

Holt sat in Spencer's chair, closer to Bryant. 'Why did you have a detective watching Alison?' he asked.

'Because I was going away for a week, and she'd have even more opportunity.'

'But it was the week of the Brussels exhibition,' Holt said.

'So?'

'I was *with* you, for God's sake! I thought it was me you suspected?'

Bryant shook his head. 'I didn't know who it was. I only found out it was you after she died.' He smiled sourly. 'It explained why Allsopp came up empty,' he said.

'But that was in March,' Holt said. 'I wasn't *having* an affair with Alison. That day — the day she died — was the first time. The only time.'

Bryant said nothing.

'It didn't occur to you that he failed because she wasn't having an affair at all?' Holt nipped the end of his cigarette.

'No,' said Bryant. 'It didn't.'

'Couldn't that be the explanation?'

'No. What does it matter now?' Bryant made to stand up, but Holt was at his side, his hand on his shoulder, exerting just enough pressure to make him sit down.

'Not yet,' he said, sitting on the table, his legs barring Bryant's escape route. 'I haven't finished.'

Bryant smoothed back what was left of his hair, and didn't speak.

20

'Allsopp,' Holt said. 'Did you employ him again?'

'No.'

'They said in court that he had left the agency,' Holt said. 'Did you employ him direct? Was he watching Alison that day?'

'He wasn't watching Alison,' Bryant said hotly. 'No one was. She probably made it up.'

'Why?'

'It may have amused her.'

'She didn't seem very amused,' said Holt.

'All right, she was mistaken. But no one was watching her. I employed the Watch agency for one week during March, and they assigned Allsopp. That was *all*.'

'Did you employ him to investigate Alison's death?'

'Of course not.'

'All right,' said Holt. 'So we accept the theory that he felt he must have missed something when he was watching her, and decided to re-investigate?'

'Presumably,' said Bryant, guardedly.

'So he found something out later, after Alison had died.' Holt relit the cigarette, and put out the match, blowing smoke into Bryant's face as he did so. 'And he got too close,' he said.

'Of course he did. He wrote to you, and you thought he was on to you.'

'I thought he could *help*. I think that's what he was trying to do.'

'This is it? This is your attempt to convince me that I should help you?'

'He's dead,' Holt said. 'And I didn't kill him. He was killed because he knew something, and I want to find out what that was.' He moved away from the table. 'And you know more than you're saying.'

Bryant got up and went to the door. 'I can't stop you playing this charade,' he said. 'But I can ask you to leave.'

Holt walked out past him. Bryant wasn't being truthful with him. He'd swear he wasn't.

'But Bill,' said Bryant.

He turned.

'If you really didn't do it, then you'd better be very careful.'

21

A threat? Or a piece of honest advice? Holt didn't know yet. But he would.

He left, and checked into the hotel. José, the manager, was friendly and talkative, and Holt found himself making conversation. It was difficult, after all this time.

At least the George hadn't changed. It was still the same old solid building, with old solid furniture. Only José and Maria, Spanish and hospitable, were new. And they seemed to be making the place popular, judging by the number of people in the bar.

He went up to his room, and re-read Allsopp's reports for the week that he had been watching Alison.

'Monday, 16th March 1970. Subject left home at . . .'

What had Allsopp discovered, months later, when he had really looked?

'Mr Harmer, I understand that Michael Allsopp was employed by you from August 1969 until March 1970. Is that correct?'

Holt looked round the courtroom. Old, wood-panelled, reeking of Victoriana. The jury, in two rows of six; the judge looking as though he'd been built in with the bench. It was hard to imagine him leaving the court and getting into a Daimler or whatever it was that judges drove. If they drove. It was hard to imagine him going to the cinema, or eating a banana.

The public gallery, packed as usual for this local rich boy gets his come-uppance show. People who had only seen Alison as the lovely girl whose face was all over the local paper. Who didn't care what she had done to him, because whatever it was, he must have deserved it. And they had decided, and the judge had decided, and the jury had decided, already.

What chance did he have? In the dock, with a policeman on either side, he looked guilty before he started. What chance did he have?

'Michael wasn't fond of the work,' Harmer was saying.

That's right, thought Holt. Call him Michael.

'He wanted to know when he'd get to do some real detective work. But you don't really get that, you know. That's just in

22

books. Except maybe a missing person now and again, but the Sally Army does that for nothing.'

'The Salvation Army, your honour,' said the prosecuting counsel.

'I am aware of that, thank you,' said the judge.

'So Mr Allsopp was keen on the idea of being what he thought of as a "real" detective?'

'Oh yes.' Harmer smiled. 'But I'm afraid that most of it's just chasing debtors and serving writs. And some divorce work still; not as much as before the law changed.'

'And during March 1970, Mr Allsopp was employed to watch Alison Bryant?'

'Yes,' Harmer said. 'Surveillance, we call it. Yes. Just for one week: the 16th to the 22nd. While Mr Bryant was away on business.'

Copies of Allsopp's reports were passed around to everyone who mattered. Holt didn't matter.

'As can be seen,' said the prosecuting counsel, 'the reports did not in fact confirm Mr Bryant's suspicions.'

'Of course they didn't,' interrupted Harmer. 'Because he was away *with* Mr Bryant!' He pointed to Holt as he spoke.

The judge told Mr Harmer that he must only answer questions put to him, and instructed the jury to disregard Mr Harmer's remarks. Great. They'd forget all about it, just like magic. The prosecuting counsel looked pleased.

'I understand that you spoke to Mr Allsopp following the death of Mrs Bryant. What was Mr Allsopp's reaction to that event?'

'He was very upset. Very. He thought that if he had found out what Mr Bryant had wanted to know, Mrs Bryant might not have died.'

'Did he seem in any way alarmed, or afraid for his own life?'

'Oh, no. He was just very upset. I don't think his heart was in it when he was watching Mrs Bryant; he left just after. I think he felt he'd missed something. He wanted to do real detective work, and if you ask me — '

'No one has asked you, Mr Harmer,' said the judge.

23

The restaurant was busy for dinner, and Holt ate heartily, now that his plan had begun. He wasn't sure that Bryant was being straight with him, but even lies helped, if you knew how to use them.

'Are you Bill Holt?'

He looked up from his coffee to see a girl: early thirties, dark hair and brown eyes. She wore denim jeans and jacket, and a blue shirt, open at the neck. The sleeves of the jacket were turned back, and she was brown with the sun.

'Yes.'

'Do you mind if I join you?'

Holt made a gesture which indicated his indifference, and she sat down.

'Jan,' she said. 'Jan Wentworth.'

He didn't speak, but poured himself some more coffee.

'I'm staying here,' she said. 'I'd like to talk to you.'

'Why?'

'Because the last time I saw you, you were shivering with cold, hanging on to the roof of a prison, and shouting that you hadn't killed anyone.'

Only reporters had been there. 'Go away,' he said quietly, and she went.

His mind went back to the days on the roof. He hadn't really been aware of the bitter temperature, warmed by the vain and foolish hope that people would know he must be innocent, or why would he do it? And knowing, inside, all the time, that he would just have to come down again. Eating what scraps of food the others could get to him, clinging to the slates, shouting until his voice deserted him and his lonely perch grew less and less newsworthy. Aware that all he'd get would be more time to spend in prison.

He left the hotel, and drove out towards Leicestershire, wanting not to do it, having to do it. 'Get up on *their* bloody roof,' one of them had said. Someone had, since then. Some other poor bugger protesting his innocence. He drove for thirty miles, until he could see it.

A ring of lights in the middle of nowhere; a ring of powerful

24

lights that seemed almost welcoming unless you knew it was a prison. A ring of lights for the cameras that watched everything. Penning men in, circling round them, watching them. And he thought about the plan that had been conceived within their glow. No trouble, he'd said, and there would be no trouble, because now he knew how to kill, and where to kill, and when to kill. He stared at the lights until they blurred and danced before his eyes.

All he had to discover was who to kill.

Three

When he got back, he went to the Green Man, a suitably sleazy pub for an ex-con to frequent. It had the added attraction of never having been frequented by anyone that he knew.

His first drink. This was a moment you were supposed to savour, but he could only enjoy his plan. 'A pint,' he said. 'Bitter.' The juke-box pounded in his left ear. It had videos playing on a screen above it. Space Invaders howled and exploded to his right.

'Can I have a drink with you?' said a woman's voice.

God, he'd forgotten that particular hazard of the sleazy pub. He didn't turn round.

He took his pint, beginning to get used to everything costing five times as much as he'd expected. So would she, presumably, but he wouldn't be availing himself of her services. He didn't want a woman. Alison had provided an acute form of aversion therapy which had stood him in good stead, as things turned out.

He had managed without female company for sixteen years, he could manage for another sixteen. For ever.

'I'll settle for a glass of water.'

'Find another customer,' he said, still not looking. 'I'm not interested.'

He turned to see Jan Wentworth.

'Do I look like a prostitute?' she asked.

'I don't know,' he said. 'I don't know what they look like these days.'

'Same as ever,' she said cheerfully. 'Too much make-up, too tight skirts, too high heels. They don't go to work in a pair of old jeans.' She smiled. 'Gin and tonic,' she said to the barman.

When it arrived, Holt took out his wallet. 'I'll get that,' he said.

They sat down and regarded one another, like boxers in a ring. He sipped the beer. It was good.

26

'Are you going to talk to me, or just stare at your pint?' she asked.

'What difference does it make?'

'Because if we're going to talk, I'd rather we went somewhere else,' she said, above the noise.

He finished his pint in a fashion of which his erstwhile colleagues would undoubtedly have approved, and stood up. She followed him to the door, having knocked back her gin with equally commendable speed.

Out in the soft, warm night, she walked past him, then turned and faced him, hands in pockets, walking backwards when he didn't stop. 'Why aren't you interested?' she asked.

He frowned. 'What?'

'Just now,' she said. 'When you thought I was soliciting. I thought men out of prison leapt on the first woman they saw.'

'Not this one,' he said. 'I don't need it, and I don't want it.'

She smiled. 'I wasn't offering,' she said. 'I just wondered.'

He stopped walking. 'Were you one of these reporters?' he asked. 'At the prison?'

She nodded, and he walked away.

'Where are we going?' she called.

'You don't seem to need to know.' He got into his car, and drove off, back to the George. He glanced in his mirror now and then to check; she was behind him.

He parked with some difficulty in the small, cramped car park, and went into the lounge, where he ordered a whisky and a gin and tonic. She came in as he sat down, and he indicated the drink, complete with ice and lemon this time.

'Thanks,' she said, sitting opposite him, picking up her glass. 'That's better,' she said.

'Do you have anything else to wear?' he asked.

She looked down at herself, and then up. 'Yes,' she said.

'Then why don't you wear it?'

She got up and left the lounge. When she came back, she was wearing a light, printed-cotton dress.

'All right?' she said.

Holt took a reflective sip of his drink.

27

'Why did you do that?' he asked.

'You asked me to.'

He pointed with his glass towards the barman. 'Would you have changed if he'd asked you to?'

'No.'

'Because he can't give you a story?'

'Neither can you. You're not news any more.'

'Then why change your clothes for me?'

'Because they were bothering you,' she said. 'I could see that. I realise why now.' She handed him a cutting from a paper. It was a photograph of him in his prison denims, up on the roof, making a fool of himself. He read the article, glancing up at her now and then.

'Very sympathetic,' he said.

'Not much help though.' She took the article back. 'I went every day. Until you came down.'

Holt frowned. 'I didn't see you.'

'They wouldn't let me stand where you could see me,' she said.

It figured, thought Holt. 'Why?' he asked. 'Why did you come?'

'I don't know,' she said. 'I felt maybe it would help. You. If someone was listening. I just hoped maybe the vibes would reach you.'

'They didn't.'

'No,' she said. 'What happened to you?'

'I got my hand smacked,' he said. 'And they sent me to Gartree, in the end.'

'That's what happened to the bones you walk round in,' she said.

Holt nodded.

'What happened to you? To start with you were making a lot of noise, appealing against the verdict, not taking no for an answer. Climbing roofs one minute, and then what?'

Holt didn't reply.

'Apart from a fighting incident,' she went on, 'there was nothing. No protests, no demands to see the governor, no attempts to be reclassified. What happened?'

28

Holt could feel a knot in his stomach tightening as she spoke. 'I grew up,' he said.

He didn't know what she wanted with him. Maybe she did think there was a story. But she was messing with the wrong man. She thought she was dealing with the idiot on the roof, scared out of his wits; she wasn't.

He stood up. 'I'm tired,' he said. 'Goodnight.'

He had been in his room for about half an hour when he heard the knock on the door. He looked up quickly. It was locked; he'd taken some pleasure in locking a door when the key was on his side. He moved to the door, unlocking it quietly.

'Come in,' he said, stepping to where the door would cover him.

She came in. 'Bill?' she said.

'What do you want?'

His voice, coming from behind her, startled her, and she turned quickly. 'I want to help you,' she said.

'To do what?' He closed the door.

'Prove you didn't kill anyone.'

So that's what she thought. He tapped the knob thoughtfully, as he stood in front of the door. 'What makes you think I didn't?' he asked.

'You said you didn't.'

'Everyone says they didn't. Some of them even climb on to prison roofs and say it. Do you always believe them?'

'No.'

He stayed where he was, his hand on the knob. 'Why do you believe me?'

'Because I know you.'

He frowned.

'You used to buy cigarettes in our shop,' she said.

He looked at her again, his eyes narrowed. 'Wentworth the tobacconist,' he said. 'You're one of his kids?'

'That's right.'

'So I must be telling the truth, because I used to buy your dad's cigarettes?'

She shrugged. 'You've come back,' she said. 'Why?'

'I have a business here.'

'It's done all right without you up till now.'

The knot in his stomach grew tighter.

'You came out this morning and you went straight to Greystone,' she said. 'Straight to all the people who would have brought back hanging just for you. Why?'

His hand gripped the door knob.

'And then you went on a ninety-minute round trip just to look at Gartree prison.'

That did it. He locked the door, and put the key in his pocket, as she watched him, her eyes wary.

'Why have you locked the door?' she asked.

He didn't answer; he just moved towards her, and she backed off a little. Another step, and she looked round, then back at him, stumbling over a chair as she stepped back. He kept advancing until she found herself literally with her back to the wall. He put his hands on the wall on either side of her.

'You can follow me,' he said quietly. 'You can poke and pry into my prison record, and my private life. It's your job. I can't stop you.' He paused. 'But if you print one word of what you learn, if you speak to anyone . . . ' He caught her wrists in a sudden movement that made her catch her breath. 'Then you won't write anything for a while,' he said, his voice mild, his grip hard. He let go, and turned his back on her, wheeling round again as he heard her moving.

She was behind the chair, her hands clutching it, putting protection between herself and him.

'What's the matter?' he asked, moving nearer, kicking away the chair, seeing her eyes go dark with fear as she glanced quickly towards the phone.

'Try it,' he said. 'See how far you get.' He moved to pick up the chair, and she automatically turned away, putting up an arm to defend herself. 'Don't you like it?' he asked. 'Don't you like being locked up with a convicted murderer?'

He righted the chair. 'Neither did I,' he said. 'So I went on the roof and shouted to them not to leave me in there with murderers and rapists and child molesters. But no one listened.'

He saw her relax as he spoke. He saw the light come back to her eyes. She swallowed. 'I did,' she said. 'I listened.'

'And I knew that that was how I was going to feel for the rest of my life,' he said, as though she hadn't spoken. 'That's what happened to me.'

'I listened,' she said again. 'I want to help.'

Holt sat down. 'How the hell could you help?' he asked.

'I can ask questions,' she said.

He looked up. 'Oh yes,' he agreed, running a hand through his hair. 'You can do that all right.'

'Well? I know *how* to ask questions; I know *who* to ask.'

'It got you in a tight corner just now,' he said.

'I got the answer.'

He smiled, then shook his head. 'No,' he said. 'It's dangerous. I can ask questions, and get answers. My way.'

She sat on the bed, still shaken. But she didn't give up. 'Maximum security etiquette doesn't go down too well in civvy street,' she said. 'There are some questions that have to be asked politely.'

He took out a packet of cigarettes, and shook one out. 'You think I can't ask a polite question?'

'I think it's too important to you,' she said. 'I think prison's screwed you up.'

'You know nothing about me!' he shouted, taking the unlit cigarette from his mouth. 'You don't know what prison's done to me. You don't know what I was like before.'

She watched him as he lit his cigarette. 'No,' she said. 'But I don't suppose your response to a knock on the door was to hide behind it. I don't suppose you went around threatening to break people's wrists.'

He leant towards her. 'If you've ever believed me,' he said. 'Believe that. Don't think I wouldn't do it.'

'But I don't *want* to write about you,' she said. 'I just want to help.'

He considered her. She'd found out a lot about him, and there were things he needed to know. But she couldn't help with them. 'What could you do?' he demanded, his voice disparaging. 'Can

31

you find out about Allsopp? Whether or not he was good at his job? What sort of man he was? Alison said he was watching her that day – they say he couldn't have been. Can you find out where the hell he was? Why he left the agency? That's what I need to know.'

'It was a long time ago,' she said. 'But I can try.'

He put out his cigarette, and shook his head. 'Are you afraid of me?' he asked.

'I'm not about to double-cross you, so I shouldn't end up with any broken bones,' she replied.

She wasn't part of his plan. Rule one, never alter your plan. But she was right. She could ask questions – she was a reporter, it was natural. Maybe his quarry wouldn't realise what was happening until it was too late. She wouldn't talk. She knew better than to talk. Besides, he almost believed that she had never meant to. Almost. But she had to have some reason.

'What's in it for you?' he asked.

She looked away, and he nodded. He'd get the truth out of her. She wasn't going to mess things up for him. No one was.

'When you went up on the roof,' she said slowly, 'they sent me because I said that I used to know you.' She gave him a brief smile. 'All's fair,' she said, by way of apology. 'It was my first real story; they thought it would give it an interesting slant.'

He relit his cigarette. 'You didn't write it like that,' he said.

'No.'

He waited.

'Because when I got there,' she said, looking at him again, 'and I saw you . . . ' She dropped her eyes. 'You were frozen. And frantic. And I just wanted to climb up and keep you company.'

He took the key from his pocket, and got slowly to his feet. 'It's too dangerous,' he said, opening the door. 'For both of us.'

She went out without speaking, and walked away down the corridor.

He closed the door, and locked it again. He had to get some sleep. He lay on the bed — the first real bed, a double bed, wide enough to stretch out in. He'd specified that to himself, years ago. A double room at the George. He meant to get up again, to

32

get undressed and appreciate the feel of soft sheets, but he fell asleep as he was, fully clothed.

The next morning, he sorted through the papers. They didn't seem to be much help at the moment. They never had been, he thought, remembering all the dead ends that he and his solicitor had gone chasing.

There were unidentified prints found in the Bryants' house; that had got his lawyers quite excited, until they discovered that the Bryants had had builders and decorators and God knows what all working there.

They had hoped that the time of death might clear him; he had had to get a taxi home in the end, and the taxi driver was sure of the time that he had picked him up. But the time of death, far from clearing him, merely shoved another nail in his coffin, and the taxi driver had given evidence for the prosecution.

An iron bar had been used in Allsopp's case — it was found, and since it couldn't possibly have his fingerprints on it, Holt had thought he'd won. But his legal advisers told him that it had had no prints on it at all, which merely proved premeditation.

They had advised him to plead guilty, and to cite provocation as his defence. Even they hadn't listened, hadn't believed him.

This time, he knew what to reject. He was looking for something new, something they had missed. Something that Allsopp had missed first time round, and had discovered when he looked more closely. He had re-read all the newspaper accounts, mostly from the *Courier*.

He looked up. That must be who Jan Wentworth was working for, he thought, and the knot in his stomach tightened. If he found one word in the paper about him, she'd regret it.

Reports, counsel's opinion, solicitors' letters. He spread them out, and read them all. There was nothing.

He stretched, and decided to leave the papers for a while. He'd call on Cartwright, to see if he was in more of a mood to assist him in his enquiries.

He wasn't, Holt gathered, as Cartwright tried to close the door in his face.

Holt was quicker than most. 'Just some questions,' he said,

planting himself firmly on Cartwright's side of the door.

'You have no right to come here,' Cartwright said.

Holt smiled. 'There was a time,' he said, 'when I had no right to receive letters. Or visitors. Or smoke, or eat a bar of chocolate. They were privileges. They could be taken away.'

Charles closed the door, and brushed past him on his way to the sitting room.

Holt followed him, through his exquisite hallway, with its elegant lines and tasteful prints, into his stage-set sitting room. Beethoven played, leather armchairs in pale, soft colours beckoned. Original art this time, adorning the otherwise plain walls, doubtless by someone so highly thought of that Holt would never have heard of him. Alison would have liked this room, this house. Not a carpet fibre out of place. Odd that she had married Bryant, whose desk disappeared under mounds of paperwork as he went through the day, and had been Cassie's closest friend. Opposites must attract. He thought she would have been much more at home with someone like Charles. Charles liked perfection.

Holt nodded to Susan Cartwright, whom he had never met; he recognised her from Wendy's description. He wasn't introduced.

'We're just about to have lunch,' Charles said. 'It'll have to be quick.'

'It's only salad,' said his wife. 'It'll keep.' She smiled at Holt.

'Ask your questions,' Charles said. 'I'm told the others have agreed. It's against my better judgement, but go ahead.'

Holt didn't really feel that he could, with Mrs Cartwright sitting there.

She twisted round to look at Charles as he poured himself a drink from a crystal decanter. 'I'll have one,' she said, her voice cool.

Charles splashed some more into another glass and handed it to her.

'Would you like a drink, Mr . . . ?' she asked, leaving the space at the end, obviously irritated by Charles.

'Holt,' he said. 'Bill Holt.'

'Oh.' She looked a little taken aback. 'I've heard about you,' she said.

34

'Nothing bad, I hope,' said Holt, and she actually laughed. It had been a long time since he'd made someone laugh. He answered her question. 'I'd rather have coffee, if it isn't too much trouble.'

'No trouble at all. How do you take it?'

'Black,' he replied. 'Like my humour.'

And she laughed again, much to the annoyance of Charles, and went off to the kitchen.

'I take it that's Mrs Cartwright,' Holt said.

'It is. What's so delicate that you have to get rid of her?'

'How well did you know Alison Bryant?' Holt said.

'Not particularly well. She was Bob's wife and the boss's daughter. That's all.'

'When you came to Greystone she wasn't anyone's wife,' Holt said. 'Did the thought never cross your mind?'

'No,' said Charles. 'I thought you and she were more or less engaged. If I'd realised that you weren't . . .' He sat down. 'Who knows?'

'So the thought did cross your mind,' Holt said.

Charles grew slightly pink. 'The thought,' he said. 'And only the thought. I was never a rival for Alison's hand.'

'Because you'd disqualified yourself? Did that annoy you?'

Charles lifted an eyebrow. 'Annoy me?' he asked. 'Why should it have annoyed me?'

'You'd missed out.'

'I realised that I might have had a chance,' he said. 'But who Alison Grey chose to marry had nothing to do with me. Of course I wasn't annoyed.'

'What did you think of her?' Holt asked.

'I didn't think anything much,' said Charles, his eyes widening slightly. 'I hardly knew her. She always seemed very friendly; I liked her.' He paused. 'She was probably the most beautiful woman I've ever seen. I think Bryant was paranoid because she looked like that.'

'Paranoid?' Holt queried.

'Having her followed! A detective, I ask you.' His pale blue eyes grew wider still as he spoke. Charles was angry.

Holt had obviously touched a nerve, and the anger seemed at

35

odds with his declared lack of interest in Alison. Something was making Charles angry, and Holt wanted to know what. The presence in his house of the man he believed had murdered Alison? Or something else? Holt didn't know. But anger was good. Better than fear, better than booze. In anger, the truth.

'Does that make him paranoid?' he asked.

'Yes. Why didn't he just *talk* to her, for God's sake? Why spy on her?'

Holt shrugged. 'Emotional scenes aren't in Bob's line,' he said. 'He'd want nice, clear-cut evidence.'

'Well, he certainly got what he was looking for, didn't he?' said Charles, his face pale with the anger that still boiled inside. 'Once she was dead.'

Susan Cartwright returned with Holt's coffee.

'Thank you,' he said.

She sat beside Charles on the sofa, and looked up at him.

'Charles,' Holt said, fighting the desire to use cell-block diplomacy. 'I wasn't having an affair with Alison.'

'I should have thought the evidence was pretty much to the contrary,' said Charles. 'And if Bryant hadn't used such underhand methods, he'd have discovered it a lot sooner.'

Holt shrugged. 'Where were you when Alison died?' he asked.

Cartwright sighed. 'I told the police twenty times,' he said.

'You haven't told me.'

'I was at work.'

Mrs Cartwright frowned. 'You're not trying to say that Charles had something to do with it?' she asked.

'No,' said Holt, truthfully. 'I just want to know. Bob Bryant said at the trial that he took Alison's phone call at half past six, and that he walked around to cool off. It was your evidence that got him released, Charles. I'd like to know what you said.'

Charles took a slow, deep breath. 'Bob and Ralph and I were having a meeting when Alison rang,' he said. 'Bob didn't say anything other than her name, then he just hung up and walked out. We waited for a few minutes, then went back to our own offices. Bob came into my office just before seven, and apologised for walking out.' He finished his drink. 'And that's it,' he said. 'Bob didn't go rushing off to murder Alison. Your attempt to make people think that failed before, and it will fail again. Because he simply didn't have time.'

'Who else was in the building?' Holt asked. 'Was Cassie there?'

'No. She'd gone home at half past five.' He raised his eyebrows. 'Oh, Spencer was there though,' he said. 'I'd forgotten that. I've no idea why; I mean, he didn't work for Greystone then. But I saw him getting into the lift.'

'When?'

'It was just before Bob came back. I'd looked along the corridor to see if I could see him, and I saw Spencer.' He looked a little surprised. 'I'd forgotten all about that,' he said.

'See?' said Holt. 'That's all I'm asking you to do. If people remember things they've forgotten, or didn't think were important, well, it could help me. You do see?'

Cartwright nodded briefly, and Holt stood up, still puzzled by why Charles should be so angry about Allsopp. 'Thanks for the coffee,' he said. He stretched out a hand to Charles. 'And for the co-operation.'

Charles ignored his hand. Holt kept it outstretched for a moment, then took it away. 'Maybe you'll tell me the rest some time,' he said.

It was a shot in the dark. If there was nothing else, it would do no harm. If there was, he would see the colour that came so easily to Charles's fair skin.

And he did.

Four

Thursday, and he was finishing lunch when she arrived. He hadn't seen her since the first night; he'd assumed she'd given up. She was wearing a blue skirt, full and light and floaty, and a white blouse. Her legs were bare.

'Are you still staying here?' he asked.

'No. I can't afford it. I've moved into awful digs. You have to be in before she locks the door.' She was excited, her eyes shining. 'Hurry up and finish that,' she said. 'I've got something to tell you.'

'Have you had lunch?' he asked.

'Oh, forget food! Hurry up.'

He hurried.

'Right,' she said, as they got into his room. 'Allsopp was in a pub when Alison Bryant died. The village pub where he lived. Lots of people saw him: the landlord and the GP were two of them,' she said, her eyes twinkling. 'He was there from opening time till closing time. He drank lager and lime,' she added.

Holt blinked. 'How the hell did you find that out?' he asked.

'I know who to ask,' she said.

'Did you go to the police?' he asked, his heart sinking.

'No. They wouldn't have told me.'

'Then where?' he demanded.

'Watch. The agency Allsopp worked for,' she said. 'I've been working there for the last three days.'

Holt couldn't believe her. He shook his head.

'I have! I told them I was a writer, and I wanted to use a detective agency. I said I wanted it to be authentic, so would they let me watch them working if I helped out a bit with some office work.' She smiled. 'They got a temp for nothing . . . ' She paused. 'And I got a lot of information,' she said.

The knot in his stomach grew tight. 'Not that information, you didn't,' he said.

'Yes,' she said, and a breeze floated in from the window, moving the folds of her skirt. 'Ex-police inspector Harmer told me. He owns the agency.'

'I know,' said Holt, still suspicious.

She looked triumphant. 'Well?' she said. 'I'm good, right?'

'How?' he said, still not trusting her. He sat down on the bed. 'How did you get him to tell you?'

'Talking,' she said. 'Just talking. No strong-arm stuff. I said I'd heard that one of his operatives was murdered on the job, and he said no, thank God, he wasn't working for him when it happened. And it went from there.' She smiled. 'Trade secret,' she said. 'Always make an inaccurate statement if you want an answer to a question.'

He nodded, still bemused, watching her as she went over to the window and opened it a little more. He could see her outline through the fine material of her blouse.

'There's more,' she said. 'Allsopp was not good at his job. Just didn't get results, said Mr Harmer. Didn't like the work, you see. A bit lazy, if you ask him.' She turned to see his reaction.

'Is that why he got rid of him?' Holt asked. This was more like it.

'He didn't. Allsopp handed in his notice in March. Then in July, Mr Harmer suddenly gets the police wanting to know who had been assigned to Mrs Bryant and where he lived.'

'And?'

'And he made it his business to find out where Allsopp was when Mrs Bryant died. "You can't be too careful, young lady. Allsopp knew Mrs Bryant's habits. It could have been burglary, or anything." ' She employed Harmer's north country accent, and he could hear him again, as he'd sounded in court, singing Michael's praises.

'He thought *Allsopp* might have killed her?'

'Briefly.'

'What did the police want with Allsopp?'

'Bryant had told them about Alison's phone call. And he'd said that he hadn't had someone watching her then, but that he had employed an agency earlier in the year. So, obviously, they wanted to talk to Allsopp about it.'

39

'But where did Harmer get all this information?' Holt asked.

'From his ex-colleagues, of course. And they were quite satisfied that Allsopp wasn't anywhere near the Bryants' house that day.'

Holt shook his head. 'If you'd heard Harmer in court,' he said. 'Butter wouldn't have melted in Michael's mouth. He didn't mention that he thought Michael might have done it. Great, isn't it?'

'Well,' she said. 'I suppose it's all right to speak ill of the dead sixteen years later. And I don't think he really thought that Allsopp had done it – he went to see him.'

'Yes, I know.' Holt looked at his watch. He wanted to hear what Jan had found out, but the time was getting on, and he had arranged to see Wendy. 'Look, can we leave it for now? I have to go out.'

She looked a little disappointed. 'Yes,' she said. 'Of course.'

He went to the dressing table. 'Allsopp's reports on Alison,' he said, picking them up. 'If you're interested.'

'Have I been taken on?' she asked.

He held out the papers, then drew them back as a thought occurred to him. A thought that pulled the knot so tight that it hurt.

'Weren't you missed?' he asked.

'Sorry?'

'At the *Courier*? I take it that is who you're working for?'

The honest brown eyes held his for a moment. 'Used to work for,' she said. 'I haven't worked there for three years. I don't even live here any more.' She stepped closer to him. 'I'm not an undercover agent, Bill. I'm trying to help.'

'Sorry,' he said, and it was the first time he had apologised for sixteen years.

'I'm enjoying myself,' she said. 'And I found out what you wanted to know, didn't I?'

Holt handed her the reports. 'Yes,' he said. 'You're good. And lucky.'

'Maybe,' she said, taking them, glancing at the top one. 'But people like to talk about interesting things that have happened, especially if they didn't happen to them.'

He smiled. 'Trouble is, it did happen to all the people I'm talking to,' he said. 'All but one. The one who made it happen.'

'So,' she said, turning the page, 'that should be a guide, then.' She looked up. 'Shouldn't it?'

Holt picked up his jacket. She really was very useful. And nice to have around. A lot more fun than the company he was used to keeping. 'I do have to go out,' he said. 'I shouldn't be long. You can stay, if you like. You might want to have a look at these.' He waved a hand at the bundles of papers on the dressing table.

'Here,' he said, throwing her the key without warning. She caught it. Somehow he had known she would. 'In case I'm not back when you want to leave,' he said.

He went down to the car park, hardly able to believe that he had just turned over his entire life to someone else. His room, his clothes, his papers, his key. That was his life, and he'd left it in her safe-keeping.

He was a little nervous of seeing Wendy, which was strange. He'd seen her regularly while he was in prison. But this was different. This was seeing her in domestic surroundings of which he had no part, because now she had a new husband. New! My God, they'd been married nine years. He had arranged to call while the not-so-new husband was at work.

'Thanks for coming while Jim's out,' Wendy said.

'Least I could do.'

He sat down in the neat kitchen, where Wendy had made tea and sandwiches. He could imagine the hours she would have spent agonising over that. Etiquette books didn't say much about entertaining convicted murderers to whom you were once married.

'Are you getting anywhere?' she asked anxiously.

'Difficult to say.' He had spent most of the last few days buying clothes. Lots of clothes. And the odd luxury item. But he'd spent the nights tossing and turning, and re-reading the trial papers. He didn't know where to start. Maybe Jan would help. 'Not really,' he said.

She nodded, and poured the tea.

'You look relieved,' he said. 'Don't you want me to find out?'

'Of course I do,' she said. 'But I don't think you can, not after all this time. And in a way . . . ' She sighed. 'In a way, you're right. I'd feel better if you could just forget it.'

'Forget it?' he repeated. Stopping breathing would be simpler.

'I had to come to terms with it as well,' she said. 'Oh, I know you were the one in prison − I'm not pretending I can begin to know what that was like − but I had to cope too. And I coped by . . . by accepting, I suppose. And now you're making me go through it all again.'

'Have you ever believed it was me?' he asked.

She shook her head.

'Then doesn't it bother you? That someone who killed two people is still free?'

'No,' she said. 'That was never what bothered me. Whoever did it is long gone. It's what happened to you that bothered me.'

Long gone. So that was how she had accepted it.

'I don't think whoever did it is gone at all,' he said.

'I know. You told us. But you're wrong, Bill. It couldn't have been any of them. They're our friends.'

'Your friends,' he said.

'All right,' she agreed. 'My friends. But they *are* my friends. And you're wrong.'

'Why did you want to stay with Greystone?' he asked. 'And why did you want to get on to the board, of all things?'

'Bill, try to put yourself in my shoes,' she said. 'Greystone was the only solid thing I had left. And they were good to me,' she said. 'I had to accept that they all believed the verdict, but they didn't hold it against *me*. Nor even you, really. They thought you couldn't have been . . . well, in your right mind.' She looked at him seriously. 'I think they're probably just humouring you now.'

Holt stopped chewing. He'd never really thought of that.

'It isn't easy,' she said. 'Not even now. Bob's never wanted me there.'

Holt frowned. 'Then why do it? I can understand what you mean about it being something to hold on to at the time, but why stay now if it's still difficult?'

'I don't mind making Bob Bryant's life less comfortable,' she said.

Holt was surprised. This didn't sound like the Wendy he knew.

42

'What do you mean?' he asked.

'None of this would have happened if it hadn't been for him,' she said. 'Moving to that house in the middle of nowhere, and then never being there. It would have served him right if she had been having an affair. But she wasn't. She wasn't like that. I don't believe she ever looked at another man until . . . ' She dropped her eyes. 'Well,' she said, 'until that day. You and I weren't getting on, and Alison was lonely. I can see how it might have happened.' She looked up. 'But she certainly didn't make a habit of it, with you or anyone else. I used to go over there a lot; I didn't even have to knock. So I'm quite sure she wasn't entertaining you for months without my knowing about it.'

Holt nodded. 'Why did she do it?' he asked.

'Because she wanted to hurt Bob. Teach him a lesson. And perhaps she wanted to teach you a lesson too.'

'Why? What had I done?'

'Let her marry Bob?' she said, then shook her head. 'Oh, I don't know. I'm not a psychologist.' She smiled. 'Funny,' she said. 'If I had found out about you and Alison in a more normal fashion, it would have seemed like such a big deal. But it wasn't. She was just lonely.'

Holt stood up. 'Yes, well,' he said. 'If I've never said I'm sorry . . . ' He waved a hand. 'You know.'

She went to the door with him. 'Would you have been sorry?' she asked. 'If all that hadn't happened?'

This was all getting too honest for him. 'I don't know,' he said. 'I never had time to find out.'

Jan's car was still in the car park when he got back to the hotel, and she scrambled out as he pulled in.

'I was just going to leave,' she said. 'I'm glad I didn't miss you.'

He made to go into the hotel.

'Let's walk,' she said. 'It's a lovely afternoon.'

They walked through the newly cobbled streets, through the red brick covered shopping centre. Streets with doors and shops without, Bill thought. Life seemed to have taken a very funny turn in the last few years. She moved in the general direction of the park, walking slightly ahead of him. As they walked, she told him what she'd discovered.

After the police had been, Mr Harmer had gone to see Allsopp. Funny chap, Allsopp. A loner. No family; they never traced any relatives. His money went to the state. A fair amount, considering he was quite young. But no one to spend it on, of course. Allsopp kept himself to himself if Jan knew what Mr Harmer meant. Didn't mix. And Allsopp had been upset about Mrs Bryant. Of course, she had been a lovely girl; he wouldn't have blamed Allsopp if he'd fallen for her. But it wasn't like that, really. He seemed . . . well, annoyed was the only way of putting it.

'Annoyed?'

'That's what he said.'

They went into the park, and he walked on the soft grass, making for a bench under a tree.

'It's not what he said in court,' he said.

Jan smiled sympathetically, and sat down beside him. 'Don't blame me,' she said.

Holt closed his eyes, and listened to the sounds of the children playing on the swings and see-saws, breathing in the smell of the grass, and just the merest whiff of Jan's perfume. 'Do you think he was annoyed because he hadn't turned up whoever it was she had been seeing?' he asked.

'That's what Harmer thinks,' she said, settling herself more comfortably. Her knee touched his. 'Here she was, apparently killed by her lover, and he'd sent in reports saying that she hadn't got one.'

'So he did a more thorough investigation,' Holt said. 'And he found out who it was.'

'Who do you think it was?' Jan asked.

'It might have been Cartwright,' he said, and told her about his visit to Charles. 'I'd have thought he'd have been her type,' he said, when he finished.

'Mm.' Jan looked thoughtful. 'Why did she marry Bryant, do you think?'

'Wendy thinks she was trying to make me sweep her off to the altar instead,' he said, with a smile. 'But I don't think so. I think it was just the older man thing. I was only twenty. He had more to offer.'

44

The sunlight slanted across the park, and the children's shadows grew longer. Mothers began the long warning process of 'just another five minutes, Justin', and he and Jan didn't speak for a while. But she couldn't go too long without asking a question.

'Would it upset you very much to go back to the Bryants' house?' she asked.

'Christ, I don't know,' he said. She was good at finding the parts other people didn't reach. 'Why?'

'You might remember something.'

He sighed. 'Oh, I'd do that all right.' He gave her a brief smile.

'Will it be too difficult?' she asked.

He shrugged. 'I don't know. Do you know what happened?'

'I've just been reading the transcript.'

'And you still find me not guilty?'

'I think you had a lousy defence,' she said. 'And, yes, I still find you not guilty.'

He gave her a little bow of thanks. 'But Bryant sold the house,' he said.

'No,' she replied. 'It's still on the market, technically. No one's lived in it since.'

'Doesn't surprise me,' Holt said. 'I don't know what possessed Bryant in the first place. The middle of nowhere was coined for that house.'

'And now it's unlucky,' Jan said. 'And probably haunted.'

It probably was. Holt shrugged. 'OK,' he said. 'It might help.' He looked at his watch. 'But we can't get the keys now,' he said.

She took keys from her bag, and dangled them in front of him. 'I was looking for somewhere very secluded,' she said. 'Somewhere I could do up. Somewhere not too expensive.'

'Perhaps I should go off to the south of France and let you do this on your own,' he said with a grin.

He had never thought his plan would be fun.

And it wasn't, once he found himself back in the house, with its wallpaper peeling, and its wood rotting. Down in the river valley, in a damp piece of unremarkable countryside, it had practically fallen into the ground.

'Do you think those stairs are safe?' Jan asked.

'The bannister definitely isn't. Don't hold on to it. I'll go first. Don't come up until I'm at the top.'

He made his way carefully to the landing, and she started up, the boards creaking below her step.

'You said she came up to look for something,' Jan said. 'At the trial. Didn't you?'

'Have a seat, Bill. I'll put the kettle on. Coffee all right?'

'Fine,' he said, taking a seat by the fireplace. Perhaps in winter a fire might make the place look cheerful; the empty grate made it look depressed.

She came back in. 'Kettle's on,' she said.

Holt gave her an old-fashioned look. 'Stop being so bright and cheerful and tell me what's wrong,' he said.

'I'll show you,' she said, dropping the breeziness. 'It's upstairs. I'll go and get it.'

She was gone some time; he got up and looked out of the window at the silent, empty landscape. Whatever she'd done, he didn't blame her. He entertained visions of her shoplifting from supermarkets, or secreting gin bottles in the lavatory cistern. Or perhaps she gambled; maybe she owed someone money she couldn't pay. He smiled at these extravagant notions. Trouble. What kind of trouble? He gave up. She'd tell him soon enough.

'Sorry,' she said, smiling. 'I was longer than I thought.' She sat on the sofa. 'It's . . . ' She broke off. 'Oh, Bill,' she said.

'What's wrong, Alison?' He sat beside her. 'Tell me.'

'Everything,' she said. 'Everything's wrong.'

He put his arms round her. 'Tell me,' he said again.

But she didn't tell him. Instead, he found her mouth on his, urgently demanding a response that at first he was too startled to make. He pulled away from her.

'Please, Bill,' she said. 'It should have been you. It should have been you all along.'

'Which room?' Jan asked, obviously not for the first time.

He didn't want to see that room, that window where she'd signalled her intentions to Allsopp. But it couldn't have been Allsopp.

46

Jan pushed open the door that he indicated. God. The bed was still there. Bryant had left it. He could see Alison again, feel her, taste her, hear her damned voice on the telephone.

'Are you all right?'

'I don't want to go in there.' She closed the door.

Almost sixteen years since he'd stood here, nearly afraid to follow Alison into the bedroom. Sixteen soul-crushing, heart-breaking years, because of a belated adolescent tumble with Alison Grey.

'It was a bad idea,' Jan said. 'Let's go.'

'No.' He pushed the door open again, and strode into the bedroom with more determination than was wise, given the state of the floorboards.

'Careful!' Jan shouted.

'Careful?' he roared back. 'You mean I might put my foot through the floor? Worse things than that can happen to you in here! I lost my wife, I lost sixteen years of my *life*, I lost my identity, and you tell me to be careful *now*!'

All the furniture was still there. The bedside table that had held the bloody phone which she could barely wait to use. The little writing desk by the side of the window. He moved to it, and pulled open the drawer, but it was empty. He didn't know what he'd expected to find. A clue of some sort. He stared at the drawer, half open. Perhaps he had found a clue. Perhaps he had.

He turned to Jan, and she was looking out of the window, her back to him.

He had only meant to comfort her. But now they were upstairs in the bedroom. Alison stood with her back to him, looking out of the window.

He glanced nervously round the room, at the newly painted woodwork, the neatly made bed. The little desk by the window had a writing pad and a pen holder. How like Alison. The drawer was open; that wasn't like Alison. He could see a photograph of her, in the drawer.

Over her shoulder he could see the valley. Rough browns and greens, and the grey smoke from the power station on the blue summer sky.

47

She'd changed her mind. She must have. He was turning to go when she spoke.

'Zip,' she said, without turning round.

He fumbled with her zip as awkwardly as a schoolboy. And he felt like a schoolboy, because he had never got this far with Alison, back in their teens. Alison hadn't been that kind of a girl. She slipped the dress off, and undid her bra while he kissed her neck, her shoulder. She turned, and it was strange to think that this was the first time he had seen her breasts. How innocent it had been. How innocent it seemed now, as she smiled, and called him Billy, like she used to.

'There's nothing much to see,' Jan said. 'The hillside, mostly, and it isn't very exciting. Apart from that, just grass and trees, and miles of nothing. You can't even see the river.'

'The photograph, the one the *Chronicle* used,' said Holt. 'Do you have any ingenious methods of getting your hands on that?'

'Easy,' she said, pleased that she could help. 'I remember that photograph. She was beautiful, wasn't she?'

Holt nodded. 'Yes,' he said. 'That photograph was in the drawer.' He pointed to the desk.

Jan glanced at it, and back at him.

'I think that's what she came up for,' he said. 'I think that's what she wanted me to see.'

He stood by the desk, and looked out of the window, from where you could see more of the hillside and less of anything else.

He lay back, still hardly able to believe that it had happened, and sat up, frowning, as Alison began dialling a number on the bedside phone.

'Bob?' she said, after a moment. 'I'm in bed with a friend of yours. If you want to know who, ask whoever's been following me all day.' And she hung up. 'I'm sorry,' she said, not looking at him.

He stared at her, at the phone. Then he leapt out of bed, pulled on his clothes, and left.

'I think,' he said slowly, as they left the bedroom, 'that she was

48

just going to get the photo when she saw whoever it was she did see.' He held out a hand to stop her coming on to the stairs with him, and went down slowly, thinking aloud. 'So she came back down, and . . . and seduced me,' he finished with what was meant to sound like a laugh. 'To teach Bryant a lesson, like Wendy said.'

He waited at the bottom of the stairs for Jan, holding out his hand to help her down the last few rickety steps.

'But I think she wanted me to see that photograph originally,' he said.

Jan looked a little doubtful. 'A photograph of herself?' she asked. 'Why would that mean trouble?'

'I don't know. But she was the neatest person on earth. Something must have made her leave that drawer open. Right?'

Jan banged the front door shut. 'Right,' she said.

They walked along the overgrown path, back to the car.

He half walked, half ran, in his eagerness to put distance between himself and Alison. What would Bryant do when he found out? Would he tell Wendy? Would he tell Ralph? He couldn't believe that Alison had done this to him. Knowing, *knowing* that someone was watching. And ringing Bob. Oh, my God, what a mess.

He was running towards the village proper, where there was a phone box, but when he got there he still couldn't remember any taxi numbers, and this damn box didn't have a directory in it. He rang directory enquiries.

It rang for what seemed like hours before anyone answered.

'Enquiries. Which town do you require?'

'I want a taxi,' he said. 'But I don't know any numbers.'

'Which town, please?'

'It doesn't matter. I just want . . . Oh, forget it.' He hung up. She wouldn't look up taxi numbers for him anyway.

He stood staring at the phone. He had to get home. He had to think what he was going to do. Should he tell Wendy before Bob did? What was he going to say to Bob, come to that? He couldn't think here. He had to get home. But it was miles. He pushed open the door of the telephone box, and looked round. The post office was closed, and the only living soul was a child of about six.

49

'Does anyone drive a taxi here?' he asked.

The child regarded him solemnly.

'You know,' he said. 'A taxi. A car to take people places.'

The child ran off into a house. Holt straightened up, and ran a hand through his hair. It had to be possible to get away from this Godforsaken place.

A woman came out of the house. 'Did you want something?' she asked him, eyeing him with suspicion.

'A taxi,' he said. 'Do you know where I can get one? Or a telephone number?'

'I don't know any numbers,' she said. 'We use Bert.'

'Bert? Where does he live?'

'Through there,' she said, pointing vaguely, and went back into the house, ushering the child in ahead of her.

He went through there, and found a whole estate of modern houses, looking out of place. Bert. He closed his eyes. Then doggedly, he went up and down streets, until he found a house, outside which was parked a car with a 'For Hire' sign.

Bert had knocked off for the day. He was going on holiday tomorrow. But since it seemed to be an emergency . . .

He had been home no more than five minutes when Wendy came in.

'Sorry I'm so late,' she said. 'Are you starving, or did you manage to fend for yourself?'

He couldn't face food. 'No. I'm not hungry.'

'You don't look very well,' she said. 'Are you all right?'

'Yes. I'm fine.'

'Did you pick up the wedding present?' she asked.

The bloody wedding present. If he'd remembered it, he might have got away with it. The knot in his stomach pulled. Got away with what? Got away with a brief and unexciting liaison with an old girlfriend. Spencer's bloody present.

'Spencer's a photographer,' he said, suddenly remembering the camera, always on his shoulder.

'Who's Spencer?'

My God, something she didn't already know. He felt as if he'd thrown a double six.

Five

What wilful fate had sent him Jan Wentworth? She sat curled up on the bed, surrounded by papers, or beside him in the car, legs crossed, asking questions the way other people stuck knives in you.

Not the ones he expected, the ones Wendy had asked, the police had asked, his lawyers had asked. Why didn't you go to the police? Why didn't you report what you found in Allsopp's caravan? Why did you lie when the police came to you? He had answers for them. Not good enough answers, but honest answers, in the end. He'd lied to Wendy about the present to cover up having been with Alison. He'd had no warning of her innocent question, he had panicked, and said the first thing that came into his head.

Then he had found out what had happened to Alison, and his lie had had to stand. Wendy thought he'd never picked up the present, and Bryant presumably just thought that it was something Alison had bought. The lie had kept him out of it, which was where he should have been, for surely it was Bob who had come home in a murderous rage, after that phone call? The police obviously thought that it was.

But then they had released Bob, and were looking for him. How could he go to the police then? Who would believe him? And then the letter from Allsopp, and that awful caravan, and more panic. Real, blind panic, a thick, grey mist of panic. It had enveloped him, and he'd crawled into his lie and stayed there until the police dragged him out of it.

Jan didn't ask about any of that. 'Did Alison know that your marriage wasn't working either?'

'We'd never discussed it, but yes, I'd say most people knew.'

'So she knew you'd be easy prey?'

Easy prey. Yes, that was what he had been. Jumping at the chance. Oh, yes, Alison would know that all right.

51

'When, do you think? When she offered to pick you up?'

'No. Later. After she went upstairs. She was — I don't know — different, somehow, when she came down.'

'Different how?'

And he had shouted at her, telling her that he couldn't answer bloody stupid questions about it. It had just happened. And she had shouted back, saying that he had to know why she'd done it, or he'd never know what had really happened.

'Would she have wanted to hurt you?' she asked, a different time.

'No.' No. He had done nothing to Alison.

'But you did take up with Wendy while you were courting Alison, didn't you?'

'Sort of — not really. We were really only friendly by then. Besides, this all happened eight years later.'

'Did you know she was unhappy with Bryant?' she asked, picking up Allsopp's reports, which were beginning to look dog-eared.

'Not really. I suppose I knew that he didn't spend much time with her. I never really thought about it, to be honest. But I knew she wasn't happy in that house.'

And so it went on, with Jan forcing him to dig into his memories, his feelings, his motives for everything, and it got them nowhere.

But she would never let go, picking up on Wednesday what he'd said on Monday, and carrying on as though there had been no break in the conversation.

'What did you mean, different?' she asked, as she drove back from an abortive visit to the *Courier* for the photograph of Alison. Jan's friend had forgotten all about it, but she would definitely look it out, and let her have copies by the end of the week.

'What?' he said.

Jan stopped at the unnecessary traffic lights, on an early-closing desert of a street. 'You said Alison was different when she came downstairs,' she said. 'And you got angry when I asked how.'

'It's difficult to explain; she was just different.' He thought about it. 'To start with she was nervous, but it was as if she was

52

screwing herself up to tell me something. Something specific. Something she was going to show me. Then when she came down, she seemed to have changed. She was different, that's all.'

The summer dress again, with white sandals. Hardly shoes at all; just a strip of white leather over her bare foot.

'And she told me that she hated the house, and she was miserable with Bob. But that wasn't what she'd been going to tell me. I'm sure it had something to do with that photograph.'

'Was anyone else keen on photography? Besides Spencer?'

Holt smiled ruefully. 'I was,' he said. 'Sort of.' He looked at her. 'I didn't take it,' he said.

'Why don't you ask Bryant? He must have given it to the papers.'

'I will. But not yet.'

'Are you going to see Spencer?' she asked, as the lights changed.

'Yes. But I want to have the photograph when I do.' He stared moodily out of the window at the old, tired town in her new frock. He didn't like it much. 'I think I'll see Cassie first,' he said.

'What's she like?' she asked.

Another one who hadn't figured in the transcript. 'I'm winning,' he said. 'I know more about some of this than you do.'

'I know she's your cousin,' Jan said, with a mischievous smile. 'And I know that she used to work at the London office, until old Mr Stone died, and she came into her shares. She came back here, and took her seat on the board in January 1970, and rumour had it that Ralph Grey was far from pleased about having a woman on the board.'

'All right,' he said. 'How do you know all that?'

'Because Arnold Stone was a rich local eccentric, and rich local eccentrics get obits. I did the research, and that included who he'd left his share of Greystone to, if you'll pardon the grammar. And they said that Ralph Grey wasn't happy about it, so I got interested in her.'

'When did you decide to deprive the *Courier* of your admirable industry?'

She smiled. 'I didn't. It got taken over and they dispensed with my services, along with half a dozen other people's.'

'So you went freelance?'

'I worked for a free sheet up north for a while, but it folded. So now I'm freelance. Not from choice.'

'Odd, about Ralph,' Holt said, almost to himself. 'Too late to ask him now.'

She pulled into the car park of the George, which he was beginning to regard as their headquarters. The sun had dipped below the buildings, and the car park was cool in the shade of the old hotel.

'So what's she like?' Jan asked again.

'I know her too well to answer that,' he said.

She looked puzzled, but let it pass. 'Why did you and she get the shares? What happened to your parents?' She undid her seat-belt, and twisted round to face him.

'Didn't your research tell you?'

'It would have, but I didn't have enough time.'

'Cassie's father and mother died in a road accident,' he said. 'And my mother didn't count, because I was a male child — like royalty. So Cassie and I got the shares.'

'Are your parents still alive?'

He drew in a long, slow breath before answering. 'No. My father was killed in the war. My mother's dead too, now.'

She didn't ask. He had been allowed out for her funeral, and he tried to push the memory away.

'Do you like Cassie?'

He considered the question. 'Yes,' he said eventually. 'I think so. When her parents died, she came to live with us. She was eight, I was six; we were like brother and sister, really. And Alison was the girl next door — except that next door was in the same building. We all grew up together.' He frowned. 'But I always feel as though Cassie isn't entirely straight with people. No, that's not what I mean. It's as if you only see what she wants you to see.'

'Isn't everyone like that?'

'Probably,' he said. 'Cassie went off to school, and then Alison followed her. I got packed off then too. I never felt I knew either of them as well again.' He sat back and closed his eyes, trying to remember what he used to feel about Cassie — about any of them — before he had put them all down as potential murderers.

Jan moved closer to him, and her mouth touched his; a gentle, almost accidental brush of her lips.

'I thought you weren't offering,' he said.

'I am now.'

'Don't waste your time.' He got out of the car, and walked away, hearing her footsteps coming after him as he reached the hotel.

'Am I being sent home?' she asked.

'Do what you like,' he said.

Inside, he stood irresolutely in the corridor, then made for the stairs.

She overtook him, going up ahead of him, and turning. 'Stop,' she said.

'I'm not interested.'

'Neither am I, right now. I want to ask you something.' She took his lack of response to mean that he would listen. 'What is it too late to ask Ralph Grey?' she said.

'Why he objected to a woman on the board.'

'Male chauvinism?'

'I never noticed it.'

'Men don't. Why is it too late? Is he dead?'

'No,' he said. 'But he thinks I murdered his daughter, and he wouldn't let me in to rescue him from a burning building. He's not as easily manipulated as Bob.'

'What did Alison think of him?'

'She was very fond of him. He thought the world of her.'

'I'd like to know how Spencer fits in,' Jan said. 'How did Ralph Grey come by him? A New York entrepreneur? Maybe Spencer did know Alison better than he's saying, especially if you think he might have taken that photograph.'

And she went, leaving him with that thought. He waited on the stair until he heard her noisy little car leave.

He spent another restless night, and rose early. He found himself waiting for her knock, and jumping up to open the door when it came.

Green trousers, and the white blouse that he could see through.

'Could you get me an interview with Ralph Grey?' she asked as soon as she walked in.

'Me?' he spluttered. 'You're joking.'

'Oh, you know. Through someone. Wendy, maybe,' she said, her eyes shining. 'Go on, Bill. Say I'm doing an article for a US trade journal.'

Holt blinked. 'For someone who looks so truthful, you can tell some lies,' he said, and gave a sigh of capitulation. 'All right, I'll see what I can do.'

He found himself ringing Wendy, explaining that Jan was really keen to do well for this mythical trade journal, and heard Wendy give a similar token protest, and a similar sigh, and say that she would see what she could do. It must be catching, he decided. And it was dangerous, he told himself, as he hung up.

She knew too much. If she said the wrong thing to the wrong person, she could ruin everything. But it did help to have someone there, someone he could talk to. He took the chair, and she took the bed, and they spread out the documents in which he was sure he would find the answer. Find the monster who had done this to him.

'Allsopp must have worked it out,' he said.

'Then so can we,' she answered. 'What about Cartwright? Where was he when it all happened?'

'At the office,' Holt sighed. 'And if Bryant didn't have time to do it, then neither did he.'

'Do you really think he might have been Alison's bit on the side?'

Holt shrugged. 'I think he's more closely involved than he says. I'll ask him again,' he said grimly. 'When Mrs Cartwright isn't there.'

Wendy rang back a couple of hours later, to say that Ralph would see Jan on Sunday, and Jan left to do some homework on Greystone.

She didn't come at all on Friday. He'd told José to let her up to his room if she came while he was out, but she didn't. He ate lunch alone, and missed her.

At five o'clock, he opened the wardrobe and surveyed his now sizeable collection of clothes. Funny, he'd never been interested in clothes before. Now they seemed important. What should he wear for Cassie? Clothes were part of his plan too, now. Look the part; look however they think you should look.

Then they'll trust you, he thought, as he walked up the path to Cassie's bungalow, hidden behind high, thick hedges. Even your quarry will trust you.

He stood with his back to the door after he'd rung her bell, looking at the high-rise flats that had been built in the sixties, where there used to be a piece of waste ground on which he had played football. More useful than waste ground, he conceded. Not as much fun as football.

'Hello, Bill.'

'I thought this might be the best time to catch you,' he said.

'It is. Have you eaten? I was just going to make something.'

'Not for me, thank you,' Holt said quickly, remembering Cassie's culinary efforts. Perhaps she'd improved in sixteen years, but he wouldn't risk it. Cassie showed him into her sitting room which was in a sort of hopeful clutter, as though there was still a chance of stopping it getting out of hand.

'You've found some questions?' she asked, pushing a cat off a chair, and ineffectually brushing at the hairs with her hand.

He had been right to wear the trousers he had chosen. They were the same colour as the cat.

'Some,' he said. 'But first I'd like to know why the open mind all of a sudden? I seem to remember that drawing and quartering would have been too good for me.'

'Still would, if you did it,' she replied. 'And Charles might be right: it might be some sort of unpleasant game.' She sat down as another cat stalked away indignantly. 'But I can't see what the point would be. That's why the open mind. Tea?' she said suddenly, and went off to the kitchen.

He followed her in. 'So you'll answer my questions?'

She didn't even answer that one. Just spooned so much tea into the pot that Holt doubted if even his prison-conditioned system would take it.

What was it Jan had said? Make an inaccurate statement if you

57

really want an answer? But if you didn't know the facts, you couldn't get them wrong. He settled for an instruction. 'Tell me about Alison,' he said.

'Tell you?' she repeated, glancing round at him. 'You knew her all her life.'

'I didn't know her that day,' he said.

'I'd have said just the opposite,' Cassie snapped.

'Biblically speaking? True. But if we could stop playing cat and mouse it would help. Bob Bryant says Alison was having an affair. He thinks it was me, and Charles thinks it was me. Wendy doesn't think she was having an affair at all. Where do you stand?'

Cassie poured water that hadn't quite boiled on to the mess of tea in the pot. 'I think it all got too much for her,' she said. 'Being watched, followed.'

'Did she tell you what sort of trouble she was in?' he asked.

Cassie didn't answer, and she was *pouring* the stuff she had just concocted in the teapot. 'Sugar?' she asked.

'Two,' he said. Sugar might help it go down, but he doubted it.

'Still no milk?' she asked.

'Drank it however it came in prison,' he said. But even in prison, it had not come like that. 'Do you think she was in some sort of trouble?' he asked, taking the mug. He went back into the sitting room, eyeing the plant pot as a possibility in an emergency.

'If she said she was, then I expect she was,' Cassie said unhelpfully, nudging a cat over.

'She didn't talk to you about it?'

Cassie swept her fair hair back from her face. She was a sort of splendid looking woman, Holt thought. She had been Jan's age, give or take, when he saw her last. In her forties, the age to be, apparently, these days, she looked good. He and Cassie had the same birth sign. Leo. The lion. Cassie looked a little like a lion.

'She wasn't happy with Bob,' she said.

'But what does a woman mean when she says she's in trouble?' Holt asked.

'Usually that she's pregnant and she shouldn't be,' Cassie said.

58

'Quite. But she wasn't.'

'No.'

'Did she think she was?' Holt asked.

'If she did, she didn't tell me about it,' said Cassie.

'You're fencing with me, Cassie. You know more about this than you've said. Why would she do that to me?'

She sighed. 'Look, she was unhappy. And what harm had she really done you? You and Wendy were washed up anyway, and there wasn't much that Bob Bryant could do to someone who owned twelve and a half per cent of the company.'

Holt sighed. He'd pointed that out in his defence. Why would he kill her? The prosecution had turned it around; why would he run away, in that case? If she hadn't really upset him at all? Heads they won, tails he lost. He hadn't had time for such rational thought.

'She didn't mean to hurt you,' Cassie said. 'You just got caught in the cross-fire.'

Holt picked up a cat as it passed, and held it. It was furry and warm, and something to hold on to in this crazy business. 'Got caught in the cross-fire?' he repeated.

'Yes. And I'm hungry, even if you're not, so if you don't mind —'

'You can't leave it there!'

'I can,' she said. 'I'm having trouble with this, Bill. She did what she did to you, and you killed her. I know you. If someone hurts you, you have to strike back, you have to get even. I heard the evidence, and I believed that you had killed her, and I hated you for it. And I still don't see how it could have been anyone else.'

She didn't speak for a moment, just looked at him as though she were trying to see something too far away. 'Bob thinks you had some sort of blackout and you really believe you didn't do it,' she said. 'Maybe he's right. Maybe Charles is right. Maybe Wendy's right. I don't know. I don't *know*, Bill!'

Holt held on to the cat, which purred and snuggled into his arms. They all thought he was mad. 'You said you'd help.'

'You ask the right questions,' she said, 'and I'll answer them.'

59

End of interview. Holt put the cat down.

The right questions, he thought, as he drove home, as he ate dinner, when he finally went to bed. The right questions.

He woke next morning from a dream-broken sleep. Talk to each of them in turn, he had thought. Pool the information, for they all *had* information — unconsidered, irrelevant, unimportant — that they had kept to themselves. He still had to see Spencer, and there were unanswered questions there.

But he had learned that he had to ask the right questions.

He had learned that they might all be afraid of him, afraid of what he might do.

And he had learned that Jan Wentworth could burn her way into his dreams, and he didn't want that.

Six

It was late Sunday afternoon before he saw her again. A cream silk blouse, tucked into a brown skirt. Tights. Shoes. An outfit he hadn't seen before. It made her look efficient. She gave him the photograph of Alison; he hadn't been prepared for how it would make him feel.

Now, she sat curled up on the bed, shoes kicked off, her legs tucked under her. He was sitting by the dressing table, listening to a tape on her cassette recorder.

'*Which magazine did you say?*'

Such a long time since he'd heard Ralph Grey's aggressive voice. He must be well into his seventies now.

'*The "Wisconsin Business Digest",*' Jan's voice said helpfully. '*It's for their British week.*'

'*Never heard of 'em.*'

'*Our readers have heard of Greystone,*' she said. '*And we'd like to know a little about the American connection: your association with Jeff Spencer.*'

Holt glanced at her. 'Thank God you didn't attempt the accent,' he said, stopping the tape.

She smiled. 'I wouldn't know a Wisconsin accent from an eightsome reel,' she said. 'I'm their British correspondent.'

He started the tape again, then stopped it. 'Does the *Wisconsin Whatsit* exist?' he asked.

'I shouldn't think so. I made it up.'

He started the tape.

'*What about him?*' Ralph demanded, in tones that used to strike fear into his underlings. Not, it would appear, into Jan.

'*Well,*' she said, and Holt could see how she looked as she spoke the word, and smiled to himself.

'*What our readers would be interested in is how Jeff Spencer did it, to be brief. We're currently running a rags-to-riches series, and*

61

Mr Spencer's success in Britain is just right for the British Week edition.'

'*Then why aren't you speaking to him?*' Ralph barked.

'*I find you get a truer picture of a man if you speak to his friends and colleagues,*' Jan said. '*No false modesty; no false claims.*'

Holt switched off again. 'This is you thinking on your feet?' he asked.

She nodded, and he felt proud of her.

'*What do you want to know?*'

'*How does a boy from the back streets of Brooklyn end up in a British board room? How does a New York go-getter meet the chairman of an old-established British business?*'

Ralph made a noise that Holt recognised as his laugh.

'*He could see how things were moving in business machines. And he preferred to be a big fish in a small pond; too much competition in the States. So he came here, and looked for someone who was making computers. He bought them out. So he had a product, but no name. We had a name, and he convinced us we needed his product.*'

'*So he picked Greystone at random?*'

'*Not Jeff Spencer,*' said Ralph. '*He does nothing at random, young woman.*'

Holt winced.

'*He examined the market. You do nothing at random, not if you want to survive. That's why he's where he is, and why you are where you are, scratching a living writing for American magazines that no one's ever heard of.*'

Jan winked at him, as the Ralph laugh barked again.

'*He wrote me a letter; I've still got it. It marked a turning point in history; not just Greystone's history. Real history. The technical revolution. He said he was using a portable typewriter now, but that soon it would be a portable computer, and Greystone would be in the vanguard.*'

Holt looked over at her; she wasn't looking at him. Ralph would certainly have approved; no jeans or bare legs today. She had done her homework.

'*Computers small enough to sit on desks, small enough to put in*

62

your pocket,' Ralph was saying, and Holt gave his attention to the tape again.

'Computers powerful enough to type letters, to plan your long-term strategy, to design automobiles, he said. And it interested me, young woman. It interested me. Then he rang up and asked to speak to the guy in charge. I liked that.'

'And how did he convince you, Sir Ralph?'

'He was offering me know-how, and a factory that was ready to go, producing calculators with our name on them. He brought a calculator for me to see.'

There was a pause. Holt could hear Ralph's footsteps. 'Where's he going?' he asked.

Jan smiled. 'He's coming round to my side of the desk,' she said. 'We were in the study.'

'I'll tell you something, young woman. He did it all on money borrowed on the strength of Greystone's interest, before he'd even seen me. Now, I didn't know that, not then. Not the sort of thing you talk about until you've pulled it off. But that took guts. Real guts. And that's what I saw. Guts, and determination, and confidence. That's how you go from back streets to board rooms. Guts.'

'Thank you, Sir Ralph. Would you mind if I asked a couple of more general questions?'

'Such as?'

'Your attitude to the modern woman. As you probably know, American women are rather more prominent in business than their British counterparts. What are your feelings on the liberated woman?'

'Bloody silly word. You talk about being liberated, you're putting yourself in a subordinate position before you start. My wife and I started our first business as equal partners; never occurred to us to do it any other way. There are too few women in industry in this country, but it's their own fault. They don't put themselves forward enough.'

'Thank you. One more question, if I may.'

'My God, you've got more questions than that damn game.'

Holt laughed. 'He doesn't know the half of it,' he said.

'*Greystone Office Equipment is one of the largest businesses in the UK still under private ownership. Is that still a good idea?*'

'*Certainly it is. Let the public get their hands on your shares and the next thing you know you've been taken over by a soft drinks company.*'

Holt laughed again. He had always liked Ralph.

'*I don't expect it will stay that way now,*' Ralph continued, sounding almost wistful.

'*Oh? Do you expect to go public?*'

'*If other people have their way, yes.*'

'*And will they? You don't have a controlling interest any more?*'

'*Never did. Equal partners with my wife, as I said. Then Arnold Stone and I formed the Greystone Company; there were thirty subscribers. We had a controlling interest between us, but when he died, that got divided up. So I'll have to bow to the wishes of the majority, and they won't want to hear what I've got to say. Don't get old, young woman. The old have no influence.*'

'*Well, thank you for such a frank interview, Sir Ralph.*'

'*Is that it?*'

'*Yes, thank you.*'

'*Then why don't you switch that machine off and come for a spot of lunch with me?*'

The tape went silent.

'So there you are,' said Jan.

'He doesn't sound much like a male chauvinist pig,' Holt said. 'Or maybe he's just mellowed.' He smiled. 'Did you have lunch with him?' he asked.

'Of course.'

'How did it go?'

'Well,' she said. 'I'll know where to go if I'm ever short of a sugar daddy.'

'Spencer next,' Holt said, picking up the photograph of Alison. 'Would you like to come?'

'Yes please,' she said, slipping on her shoes.

Sunday afternoon, in the sunshine. She should be going on a picnic, or walking in the park. Or even getting mink coats and diamonds from Ralph. Not wasting her time with him.

Spencer's country cottage looked like a picture postcard of

Merrie England. Jan pushed open the wooden gate, and raised her eyebrows a little at the roses round the door.

Spencer invited them in cordially enough, and Holt barely waited for the introductions to be over before producing Alison's photograph.

'Thought this might interest you,' he said, handing it to him.

Spencer glanced at it. 'Alison,' he said. 'That's the one the papers used, isn't it?' He gave it back.

'It's a good photograph, isn't it?' Holt said.

Spencer looked a bit dubious. 'I didn't know Alison,' he said. 'So I can't really vouch for the likeness. But it's a good candid shot of a beautiful lady laughing.'

'Candid?'

'Subject unaware, they call it, sometimes. She didn't know she was being taken.'

Holt frowned. 'Can you be sure?'

'Pretty sure. Look at the depth of focus: it was taken with a long-focus lens. The camera would have been a long way off.'

'Did you tell the police that?' Holt asked.

Spencer smiled, the easy smile that always got one in response, even from Holt. 'I never saw the photo before,' he said. 'Only the reprint in the paper, and they cut all this stuff in the foreground out.' He indicated two dark shapes down either side of the shot, and gave Holt the photograph back. 'But the police would know all that,' he said. 'They do have some photographers of their own to call on.'

'Yes, of course.' Holt scratched his head. 'But no one mentioned it.'

'There probably wasn't any mystery about it,' Spencer said. He turned to Jan. 'What can I get you?' he asked. 'Something long and cool?'

Jan smiled. 'Thank you,' she said.

He was glad he'd brought Jan. Because she made him feel safe.

Spencer came back with the long cool drinks. 'I hear you're getting people on your side now,' he said.

'How about you?' Holt asked.

'I'm neutral,' he said. 'I nailed my colours firmly to the fence, as one of your politicians once said of another.'

Jan laughed, and took the photograph from Holt. 'She was really beautiful,' she said. 'The sort of face you wouldn't forget.'

Holt watched Spencer as she spoke.

'Bill says you saw her that evening at the station,' she went on.

'So I believe,' he said.

Jan glanced at the snapshot again. 'You saw her at the station on Friday evening, and by seven o'clock, she'd been murdered. By Saturday night, this photo was on the front page of the *Chronicle*.' She looked up at him.

Spencer's expression hadn't changed. He looked politely interested in what she was saying.

'I can't believe you forgot a face like that,' she said.

Spencer looked back for a moment, then smiled. He nodded, and held up a hand in surrender.

'You did recognise her,' she said.

'Sure I did. Like you said, you don't forget a face like that. I recognised her as the girl who met Bill at the station. I didn't know who she was until I read the paper, and I kept my mouth shut.'

Holt sat forward. 'Why didn't you talk to the police?'

'Are you kidding? Look, I stayed out of it. If you'd got yourself into something heavy, I wasn't going to make it any heavier. I didn't talk to anyone. Not even Thelma.'

'You didn't want to get involved,' said Jan.

'You said it, lady. Life was complicated enough without that.'

'Why were you here that evening?' asked Holt.

'I was spending the weekend with Thelma,' Spencer said.

'I'm told you were at Greystone,' Holt said, his voice hard.

Spencer frowned, then his brow cleared. 'You're right,' he said. 'I did go to Greystone.'

'Why?'

'To take photographs, would you believe?'

No, thought Holt.

'It was some competition: industry and the countryside or some damn thing. And you know the field behind the Greystone building? With the cows in it? Well, I wanted a shot of that through an office window – you know. Show the filing cabinets

66

and the sales graphs and the cows right outside the window. I went to see Ralph, to ask if it was OK.'

'What time were you there?' Holt asked, sitting forward.

'Oh, I don't know. Still a lot of daylight, but quite late. For the office still to be open, I mean. But I was passing, and I saw Ralph's car, so I went up.'

Jan set her drink down on the glass-topped table, with a click. 'Why were you so shy about telling us?' she asked.

Spencer sat back with a smile. 'Sharp,' he said. 'Hang on to this one, Bill.' He turned back to Jan. 'Because,' he explained reluctantly, 'when I saw Ralph, he asked me if I'd seen Bob. Said he'd had a phone call half an hour before, and had left the office, and they couldn't find him.'

Holt stared at him.

'Look, at the time it meant nothing. I just took my photographs, and went to Thelma's. Someone rang Thelma next day and told her Alison Bryant was dead, and I wondered then about Bryant disappearing, but I was staying out of it. And I didn't know it had anything to do with you until I saw the paper that night.'

'You bastard.'

'Come on, Bill! It made no difference to you. Bryant came back about five minutes after that — Cartwright saw him. So he hadn't really gone missing at all. If I'd had anything to tell, I'd have told it. But I hadn't.'

'Because you didn't want to upset the apple-cart,' Holt said, glad that Jan was there, or he would have hit him.

'All I knew was that there was something very heavy going on, and I didn't want to know. You bet I didn't want to upset any apple-carts. And it wouldn't have helped you if I had, would it?'

Holt took a deep breath. It was true. Spencer's story wouldn't have helped. 'All right,' he said, and picked up the photograph again. 'Do you think Allsopp could have taken this?' he asked, trying out his theory on the photograph for the first time.

Spencer lifted a non-committal hand. 'Might have done,' he said.

'Suppose Alison found this in Bryant's desk or something?

Realised that someone was taking photographs of her? She might have called that trouble.'

'She might,' Spencer said. 'But anyone could have taken it.'

'Without her knowing?'

'Sure. Lots of people do it — I do it.'

'Did you take this one?'

'Oh, come on.' Spencer ran a hand over his face. 'Am I a suspect?'

Holt didn't answer.

'I never met her,' Spencer said. 'OK?'

'I know you say you never met her. What puzzles me is where you were, Spencer.'

Spencer frowned. 'When?'

'Between getting off the train, and arriving at Greystone.'

'I was taking photographs,' he said. 'For the competition. Pylons crossing meadows, the power station through the trees. No witnesses, I'm afraid. I was way out in the country.'

'What did you mean, anyone could have taken it?' Jan asked.

'You pick faces out of a crowd, at a football match, or a funfair. You get good shots. She could have been on a beach somewhere. Beach photographers do it — they pin the photos up. You see one of your girl, you buy it.' He stood up. 'Now,' he said, 'if you don't mind.' He looked at Jan. 'I'm sorry,' he said. 'But Thelma's going to be back from her mother's any minute, and I think she'd rather Bill had gone.'

'Don't apologise to me,' Jan said coldly.

'That's the way it is,' Spencer said.

'Could I ask a question?' she said.

Holt had never thought she needed permission.

'Sure,' said Spencer.

'Where were you when Allsopp died?' she asked.

He smiled. 'I *am* a suspect,' he said. 'I'm sorry, but I've no idea.' He frowned. 'No, maybe I have. Thelma and I were at a dinner party here the night Bill was arrested. So I must have come on the afternoon train. And he died in the afternoon, didn't he, Bill?'

Holt nodded. 'Any witnesses this time?' he asked.

'A trainload. But who's going to remember after . . . what is it? Sixteen years?'

'Yes,' said Holt. 'Sixteen years.'

They took their leave of Spencer, and got back into the car.

'Well?' said Jan.

'I don't believe a word of it,' Holt said.

'Neither do I. Do you think he was Alison's boyfriend?'

'He didn't fall for my line about its being a good photograph of her,' Holt said.

'That,' said Jan, 'was about as subtle as your other method.'

Holt smiled. But he'd have used his other method if she hadn't been there. And perhaps he'd use it next time.

Seven

White jeans, and a sleeveless, collarless, pink sort of vest with two buttons at the neck, undone. She was sitting beside him in the car, poring over the road map. Holt could never read anything in a moving vehicle, and he admired her all the more.

At her request, they were on their way to the village where Allsopp had lived, or more to the point, as Jan had remarked, where Allsopp had died. Making the journey Holt had made to keep his appointment.

It had seemed so innocuous, lying on the telephone table with the rest of his mail. Just another bill, he'd thought. A small white envelope addressed to W. Holt, and not even sealed. But it might just as well have been a bomb:

> *Dear Mr Holt,*
> *I am a private enquiry agent carrying out an investigation into the death of Mrs Alison Bryant on Friday, 24th July, and I would be grateful if I could put some questions to you concerning the matter. I will call on you on Friday, 7th August at 7.30 p.m. unless I hear from you that this is inconvenient. If you prefer, you could call on me at the above address at 3.30 p.m. on that day. Follow the main village street . . .*

The letter had alarmed him, but he had hoped that Allsopp might be able to help.

He slowed down to negotiate a sharp bend in the country road. 'I couldn't have him coming to the house,' he said. 'So I went. The second biggest mistake I ever made.'

'It's left at this crossroads,' she said, consulting the map.

He signalled left. 'Where now?' he asked, as the road forked ahead.

'Right, I think. Then you should be in the village.'

He was indeed in the village, and his heart lurched with the

70

memory of that day. He pulled the car up to the kerb. So many times. He'd told so many people so many times. 'Shall we get out?' he said. 'I'd rather walk.'

Jan, unquestioning, did as she was asked, and they walked together along the village street. A breeze had sprung up, welcome relief from the sudden heatwave. She walked ahead of him, consulting her map.

'I know the way from here,' he said. It was a journey he had made a hundred times — awake, asleep. Over and over. Along the main village road, turn left at the pillar box. It looks like a dead end. Follow the path through the wood.

'Keep walking,' he said, as they turned by the pillar box, still there. 'You go on into the wood.'

She folded the map and slid it into the back pocket of her jeans. He stopped walking, and took out his cigarettes, but it was hopeless trying to light one in the breeze. He put them away. 'This is where I parked the car,' he said, when they got to the abrupt end of the road.

They went together into the leafy gloom, along a path still visible, though grassed over.

'I didn't know it at the time,' he said. 'But I've learned since. I was being fitted up.'

'Do you think someone else wrote the letter?' she asked.

'No. According to the police, there was nothing wrong with the letter. I think someone got him to write it.'

'Who?'

'That's what I'm trying to find out.'

'But even if someone did get you here on purpose,' she said. 'No one could have known you were going to Alison's. How could that have been arranged?'

He looked quickly at her as she spoke. 'Are you beginning to have doubts?' he asked.

'No,' she said.

They couldn't see the road any more. A solitary bird was calling; only its repeated notes broke the silence.

'Does being in the woods with a double-murderer upset you?' he asked.

'Don't start all that again,' she said sharply.

71

'Sorry.'

'Maybe Allsopp told someone you were coming,' she said.

It hardly seemed likely. Holt didn't respond. They walked on, following the path Holt had followed that day. Once again, he wondered if it led anywhere at all. 'It's just the same,' he said. 'Nothing's changed.'

'No, well, trees take a long time to change, don't they?'

It was hot, even in the woods; the breeze shifted the high branches, but it didn't reach them where they walked.

'This is it,' said Holt, as they came to a clearing. 'This is where his caravan was.'

Holt walked slowly up to the caravan, the door of which stood open wide, touching the side of the caravan itself. Perhaps Allsopp had seen him approach, opened the door. But how? The woods obscured the path until the last moment.

He almost tiptoed up to it, and glanced inside. Empty. The door had a heavy padlock on it; it seemed odd that Allsopp would have gone off and left the place standing open.

Inside was a bunk, a paraffin heater, and a desk and chair. The desk had a typewriter and some papers on it. Why did Allsopp want to see him? Holt licked his lips. If he could just take a look, see what he'd got on his desk, it might help. Just so that he knew why he wanted to speak to him. Where the hell was he?

He went up the steps, into the caravan, and glanced through the papers. Just documents. Personal, mostly. Holt picked up a notebook, riffling through the pages. Nothing. Where was he? He didn't know what he was looking for, damn it. He picked up the books and files that cluttered the desk, looking behind them, under them. There was nothing. Nothing. Nothing.

Except the blood.

'What did you do then?' Jan was asking.

Always asking, asking. 'I left. I went back to the car. I went home. All right?' He walked on quickly. He didn't want to stay there, and he didn't want to retrace the steps he had taken that day.

He followed the rough path, where it could still just be seen through the grass, further into the wood. Jan almost had to run to keep up with him, but he didn't slow down until they were out of the woods again, and on to a patch of roughish ground. He tried to light his cigarette again, but he was back in the breeze, and his hands were trembling.

'There's the old station,' she said, pointing. 'Along there. You can get out of the wind there.'

They walked about three hundred yards along the coarse grass, until it sloped down towards the old platform. Holt pushed one of the doors to the building, and it opened grudgingly, scraping the floor. He lit his cigarette as she came in after him.

Planks boarded the windows, and sunlight seeped through the spaces on to discarded boxes and dumped rubbish. His feet scraped on the grit-strewn floor as he walked to the bench and sat down, looking round at the cracked, graffiti-covered walls. The door was missing from the ladies' lavatory that once had been there. Everything stealable had been stolen. The tiles had been green; they were almost black.

Jan had wandered off, and he smoked his cigarette without questions being fired at him. He ground the stub out in the grime, and walked back out into the sunshine.

She was in the ticket office. She looked at him through an intact grille, and smiled. He didn't smile back. She came out and stood beside him, putting her arm round his waist, and giving him a squeeze. 'It hasn't made you remember anything this time,' she said, her voice apologetic.

'Hasn't it?' he said bitterly, walking away from her.

'Anything useful, I meant,' she said with a short sigh.

The sun climbed in the hot sky, and he wiped perspiration from his neck.

In the distance, a train appeared, the sun touching it as it silently made its way towards them. Then they could hear it, the sound swelling to a thunderous roar as it careered through the station, shaking more grit and brick dust on to the floors of the old building. The noise died away, and it turned back into a silent snake.

'Trains used to stop here,' Jan said wistfully. 'Before Mr Beeching. It was a lovely little station.'

Holt grunted.

'Suppose,' she said lazily, 'a magic train came in, and it could take you anywhere at all, where would you go?'

Holt didn't want to play silly games.

'Anywhere,' she said. 'Time, space. Where?'

'I don't know,' he said. 'Where would you go?'

'The Wild West. I always fancied myself as Annie Oakley or Calamity Jane. No long dresses. Buckskin and a cowboy hat. I'd sit round a campfire and throw the dregs of my coffee on it.'

He laughed.

'So, where would you go?'

Holt walked slowly to the edge of the platform. 'Right here,' he said. '7th August, 1970, between three and four o'clock. That's when Allsopp died. I could stroll along to Allsopp's caravan, and see who did this to me.'

Her face was serious as she came to him. 'We're finding things out,' she said.

'Like what?'

Jan looked along the track. 'Trains did stop here in 1970,' she said, frowning slightly.

Holt shook his head. 'No,' he said. 'Beeching was mid-sixties.'

'I know. But they were working on the line — on the new platforms. Remember? Some of the trains had to stop here to let the up trains through.'

'Not here,' Holt said. 'Further along.'

Jan smiled. 'If you went first class, maybe,' she said. 'But the rest of us were still here.'

Holt felt bewildered, as though someone had thrown him a life-belt and he couldn't reach it.

'I know a man who keeps records going back years if you want me to check.'

'Check what?'

'The train Spencer says he was on. See if it had to stop here.'

'No need,' Holt said. 'I was on it most Fridays. It did. But so what? How long did it stop for? A minute? A minute and a half at the most.' He wished he hadn't put her down as soon as he had spoken. 'Sorry,' he said. 'But it just didn't stop long enough.'

'I'll ask my man,' she said. 'You never know.' She paused. 'Why were you on it most Fridays?' she asked.

'I had to go to the London office on Friday mornings.'

'But not that morning?'

'No. Because I couldn't have got back in time for my appointment with Allsopp.'

'Did anyone go in your place?' she asked.

'Cartwright,' he said. 'Grumbling that he wasn't an office boy.'

'So he'd be on that train, wouldn't he?'

'Yes, I suppose so. Oh, for God's sake, what difference does it make?' he shouted, tired of her questions. 'The train didn't stop long enough!' And then he realised, and began to laugh. It was preciously close to hysteria, and he fought to bring himself under control.

'Allsopp was dead by four o'clock,' he said. 'That bloody train didn't get here until nearer five!' He had shouted the words, angry at her for raising his hopes for just a moment.

He walked away, towards the bridge. His soft shoes made no noise on the iron steps, and he could hear her coming after him. He stopped in the middle of the bridge, leaning on it, looking down the line. The metal was hot under his arms. Jan arrived at his side.

'What happened after you got home?' she asked.

'I was arrested,' he answered. 'I got taken away.' He didn't like it up here on the bridge. Everything was too hot, too bright, too shiny.

'I never saw my house again,' he said, suddenly aware of that for the first time. It shocked him; it shocked Jan too.

'No more questions,' he said.

No trouble. There would be no trouble, because no one else would know about it. Just him, and whoever did that to him. Somewhere quiet, deserted. A dark alley, waste ground. Somewhere like this. Or maybe at home, where people least suspected danger. Yes, sometimes that was best. He'd know what was best when he knew who it was. He would hunt, stalk and kill the monster who had done this to him. He was breathing hard as he thought of the moment that he'd dreamed of, when he had the

75

monster at his mercy. For there would be no mercy.

'Let's go back down,' Jan said.

They walked together down the steps, over to the bench. Holt sat down, remembering his house. Wendy had sold it. He didn't even know who lived in it. He had never thought about it until now.

Jan sat close to him. 'Bill,' she said, her voice gentle. 'Are you all right?'

'I want to see my house again,' he said.

And he drove to the house, along streets he hadn't seen for sixteen years, to the house he hadn't seen for sixteen years, and wouldn't have recognised. New door, new windows, new garage. He parked right outside, indulging in some sort of refined self-torture.

He let himself into the empty house. Wendy was still at work, and he didn't know if he was glad or sorry. The atmosphere was impossible when they were together. But he didn't like the empty house. He might have told her everything if she'd been there. About Alison, about the blood in the caravan. He needed her.

But when she did come in, he didn't tell her. He didn't speak at all, until he heard the doom-laden knock at the door, and he knew that it was all over. It was almost a relief.

'Mrs Holt? I'm Detective Sergeant Cash, and this is PC Foulds. We're making enquiries into the death of Mrs Alison Bryant. May we come in?'

They came in, and Holt was introduced.

'Sorry to bother you, Mrs Holt, but it's about a package which was found in the boot of Mrs Bryant's car. Until now, Mr Bryant thought that it belonged to his wife, but on closer inspection, he found your name on a label on the box itself.'

Holt stood up. 'I can explain that,' he said.

'Oh, good,' said the sergeant.

'Yes. You see, Mrs Bryant drove me home from the station.'

'When, sir?'

'That day,' he said, feeling the perspiration break out on his hairline.

76

'Which day, sir? The day she died?'

Holt nodded.

'I think, Mr Holt, that we'd better continue this conversation at the police station. Don't you?'

They had driven back to the hotel when he had had enough torture, and now she sat on his bed, surrounded by notes on the trial, her notebook filling up with pieces of information that she thought might help. He sat beside her, on a chair by the bed, reading and re-reading Allsopp's reports. He put them down on the dressing table.

'The whole thing's crazy,' he said. 'We've picked the only people who can prove that they were nowhere near Allsopp when he died.'

Jan looked up, her face almost stern. 'Spencer can't prove it. He said so himself.' She sighed. 'But Bryant's a whole lot more likely than either Cartwright or Spencer.'

'Bryant didn't want Alison dead,' Holt said. 'Not before the phone call, anyway. And he didn't have time after it.'

'He came into all the shares that her mother had left her,' Jan said.

Holt yawned. 'They might be worth killing for now,' he said. 'But they weren't then. Even if people outside books did kill for that sort of thing.'

'They do,' Jan said, injured, then glanced at the clock. 'Is that the *time*?' she said, with what seemed like genuine horror.

'Ten past twelve,' he said, looking at the very expensive watch he'd bought himself as a coming-out present.

'Oh, my God,' she said, her hand at her mouth. 'I've been locked out.'

He made a dismissive noise. 'No, you haven't. Knock on the door.'

'No! I've been locked out, really. "A minute past eleven, miss, and you'll find that door bolted," that's what she said.'

'You'll have to get a room here, then.'

She gave him an exasperated smile. 'Come on,' she said. 'You've had a hard day. Let your hair down.'

'No thanks. I don't want to let my hair down.'

She shook her head. 'Alison Bryant is not typical,' she said. 'You can trust some women.'

'I know. I trust you. I trust you more than I thought I would ever trust anyone again. I don't want to sleep with you.'

'Why not?' she asked.

'Because I don't need it. Go and get a room.'

'It's too expensive.'

'I'll pay. Go and get a room.'

'I'll sleep in the chair. I won't come near you.'

'Go and get a room.'

She sighed, and slid off the bed, taking some time over finding her bits and pieces.

'They won't run away,' he said. 'You can leave them here.'

'No,' she said, sweeping them into the briefcase which she had taken to using for the paperwork. 'You don't want anything cluttering up your bed.' She snapped it shut and went to the door, then turned.

'You'd enjoy yourself,' she said, with a smile, then held up a hand. 'I know,' she said. 'I'll go and get a room.'

Eight

'Can I ask why I'm here?' Jan said, as Holt took the car into Greystone's car park. Shadow engulfed them, which seemed all too appropriate.

'I don't really know,' he confessed. 'I'd just like you to talk to Bryant.'

'What about?'

'The weather, if you like. Anything. I want to know what you think of him.'

He wanted to know what Jan's instincts told her about him. He'd watched her with Spencer, and she'd warmed to him, even though she couldn't be sure of him. She had relaxed, and laughed if he did. She had said that she had found him attractive, but that she felt as though she was watching someone play a part. And he wanted to know how she found Bryant.

Waving aside Bryant's secretary's protests, he knocked on the adjoining door, and breezed into Bryant's office.

'I've brought someone to meet you, Bob,' he said.

Bryant looked a little bewildered by this invasion of his office. His was the executive suite: studded leather chairs which matched the leather-topped desk on which papers were strewn. On the other side of the room was a table, a small version of the board room table next door. A table for all those working parties and steering committees to sit round; had he really once been a part of that?

'Jan Wentworth,' he said, with a nod in Jan's direction. She was wearing the blue skirt and white blouse today. He hoped Bryant appreciated it.

'How do you do,' Jan said. 'It's very good of you to see me.'

Bryant blinked a little, and took off his reading glasses. 'How do you do,' he replied automatically, standing up and shaking hands. 'Can I help you with something?'

'I'm a journalist,' she said. 'I recently spoke to Sir Ralph Grey

79

— it was for an article I'm doing for an American trade journal.'

'Oh?' He smiled a little uncertainly.

'I wondered if you could give me a few minutes of your time?' Jan asked.

'Well, I'm a bit . . .' He looked at the paperwork, then back at her, and smiled again. 'I expect it can wait,' he said. 'Ralph mentioned your visit.' He glanced over at Holt. 'I don't think he realised that you —' he began.

'I'm sure he didn't,' Holt said. 'Don't worry. I'm not staying.' He left the office, having seen what he wanted to see.

He hadn't made any suggestion to Jan as to her approach; she had forestalled the introduction that he might have made, and gone into her journalist act. Which meant that Bryant was arm's-length material.

He wanted to interview someone too, and he walked briskly along the corridor to Charles's office. He by-passed any hostile reaction from over-loyal secretaries by knocking directly on the corridor door, and found Charles alone.

'Bill,' Charles said, surprised but civil.

It was as close to a friendly greeting as he had yet received, and he walked into the office, unsure of the tactics he intended to use.

Cartwright's office looked out on to the fields that Spencer had been so taken with for his photographic competition. A cow or two ate placidly at the grass even as he looked, and he wished he were a cow. A cow, not a bull with its horns and its aggression. A cow, eating grass.

The office was, of course, the successful businessman's office. One or two good but inexpensive pieces of modern sculpture, a complex executive toy, a calendar which must have cost the earth, and just told you the date, like any other. Greystone's leap into the big time that had come with the gutsy Spencer had done Cartwright no harm. Holt didn't sit.

'I got the impression that there was more,' he said, deciding that it would have to be cell-block diplomacy, even if Cartwright was being civil.

Charles laid an elegant hand on the desk, moving his diary a fraction of an inch. Alison used to do that, Holt remembered. Things had to be exactly where they were supposed to be. He

80

thought that if anyone would have appealed to Alison, it would have been Cartwright.

'More what?' asked Cartwright.

'Something you weren't telling me.'

Charles looked puzzled, and Holt walked round the desk, standing behind him. A simple manoeuvre that he'd learned from the police. Charles now had the choice of staring straight ahead and speaking into thin air, not speaking at all, or twisting round into a subordinate position. Or he could get up, which was why Holt now laid his hand on Cartwright's shoulders. Now, he could only get up if he removed his hands. They just rested lightly, but at the hint of movement, their pressure would increase.

'Suppose you tell me now,' he said.

Charles chose not to speak.

'You see,' Holt went on, 'something puzzled me when we last spoke.'

'And what was that?' Charles chose to address the empty office in front of him.

'You get very angry when you talk about Alison,' Holt said. He tapped Cartwright's shoulders. 'Don't you?' he asked.

There was silence, and he could see the flush rising on Cartwright's neck.

'See?' said Holt. 'Odd, isn't it?'

'I don't think so,' said Cartwright. 'She was twenty-eight years old, she was beautiful, and someone did an appalling thing to her.'

Holt nodded. 'Good reasons to get angry,' he said. 'Very good. But that's not what you were angry about — what you're still angry about.' He bent down and whispered in Cartwright's ear. 'Is it?'

He stepped back again, out of Cartwright's line of vision. 'Do you think I was having an affair with Alison?' he asked.

Charles didn't answer. Holt saw his hand move toward the intercom, and caught his wrist. 'Let's not involve other people,' he said.

'Let go,' said Charles, trying to pull his arm away.

Holt released it suddenly, so that Cartwright hit himself.

'Don't worry, Charles,' he said. 'You're quite safe here. With your secretary to protect you.' He caught the chair and swivelled it round so that Charles was looking at him. 'It's when you go home that you have to worry,' he said. 'It's dark down there in the car park. And all those muggers in the streets.' He tutted. 'It's a violent society we live in these days. Or so I've been told.'

'Are you threatening me?' Charles asked, his face tight.

'Yes, Charles. I've picked up some very anti-social habits. And if you don't tell me whatever it is you're keeping to yourself, I'll introduce you to some of them.'

Cartwright didn't drop his gaze.

'Me,' Holt said. 'And Alison. That's what makes you angry, isn't it, Charles?' He sat on the desk. 'Why, Charles?' he asked. 'Why should you give a damn who was screwing Alison?'

Cartwright's face grew tight and pale. 'Because I wasn't,' he said. 'But Bryant believed I was.' He pushed his chair back, further away from Holt. 'I could have been chief executive,' he said. 'Maybe even as young as thirty-five, certainly by the time I was forty. Thanks to you,' he said, 'and Alison, that never happened.'

Holt ran his finger along the edge of the blotter, moving it slightly. 'So that's why he's paranoid,' he said. 'Because he accused you of playing around with his wife?'

Cartwright was shaking his head. 'Because he accused every-one except the right person,' he said. 'And that was you.'

Holt didn't bother to defend himself. 'Everyone?' he asked.

Cartwright relaxed slightly, and pulled his chair closer to the desk again. 'Remember young Warwick?' he asked putting the blotter back where it belonged.

'Of course I do,' Holt said. He was hardly likely to have forgotten young Warwick who had never had the chance to be anything other than young.

'Bryant had arranged a Saturday meeting with Jeff Spencer,' Cartwright said. 'And then he found he had to be in Brussels that weekend. Remember?'

'Yes.' Holt looked at the cows.

'So Ralph and I were to meet him instead, and Warwick was

there to take notes for Bryant to read when he got back.'

Holt wished he was a cow.

'Spencer didn't turn up. Alison did — looking for Ralph. She came into my office, and Warwick turned red and left the room. I went after him and he told me he was embarrassed because Bryant had warned him to stay away from Alison. He swore he'd never had anything to do with her.'

Holt turned. 'What made Bryant think it was Warwick?'

'According to Warwick, he took her home one day when her car was being serviced,' Cartwright said. 'That was all. And I believed him. The boy didn't know what was going on. I tell you, the man was paranoid about her.' He shook his head. 'I told Warwick he could go, since Spencer obviously wasn't coming. I've always felt responsible for the accident.'

If he was looking for the usual platitudes, he'd come to the wrong shop. Holt didn't care what weighed on Cartwright's conscience, unless it was murder.

'We found him when we went down,' he said. 'Not five minutes later.' He cleared his throat. 'Someone had called an ambulance, but . . . ' He finished the sentence with a lift of his eyebrows.

'Didn't you hear anything?' Holt asked.

'No,' he said. 'We were all in here.' He sighed. 'And then Warwick was dead. But Alison was still giving Bryant cause for concern. So he moved on to me.'

Holt sat down again. 'Go on,' he said.

'The house-warming,' Cartwright said. 'I'm sure you remember the house-warming.'

Holt grunted. No one could forget that dismal night. 'You left early,' he said to Cartwright. 'You missed the worst part.'

'I caused the worst part,' said Cartwright.

'How?'

'I was leaving,' he said. 'I went up to get my coat from the bedroom, and Alison was in there. Bryant came out of the bathroom, and saw us.'

'What were you doing?'

'*Nothing!*' Cartwright said fiercely. 'We were laughing about something, and that was enough. The next day, he told me I could forget about being considered for the chief executive position.' He leant over the desk. 'Because he thought *I* was screwing Alison, as you so delicately put it.' He sat back again. 'He told me he thought I was too young to take the responsibility, and too interested in his wife.' He paused. 'Paranoid?'

Holt shrugged.

'No,' said Cartwright. 'I didn't suppose you would agree, since you were the one who was making him paranoid. But Alison had to die before Bryant found that out.'

Holt began once again to protest his innocence, but froze in mid-word, as a terrible thought occurred to him. Too terrible to voice. He stood up again. It was nonsense, anyway. Utter nonsense. He looked out at the cows, standing, sitting, eating, sleeping. Not knowing, not caring.

'Why did you stay on at Greystone?' he asked.

'Because of Spencer,' Cartwright answered without hesitation. 'I hitched my wagon to Spencer's star. Why not? I knew he'd be good for us.'

'But you're still working for Bryant. And you're still not chief executive.'

'Ambitions change,' Cartwright said. 'This firm will go public within twelve months.' He spoke carefully, measuring his words. 'It's taken a long time; I had to wait for Ralph to retire of his own accord, because no one was going to oppose his re-election, however decrepit he got.'

He hadn't seemed decrepit, Holt thought, rubbing his eyes. 'So you're the one who was pulling Wendy's strings,' he said. 'That's why you got her on to the board.'

'That's right. And shortly after we've gone public, you will be made a substantial offer for your shares by another major company. The board will recommend that you accept.'

Wheeling and dealing were never Holt's forte, and he'd been away too long. 'What?' he said.

'Even if Cassie supports Bryant — and she might, being a Stone — Wendy won't, and neither will Spencer. So the board will recommend that the shareholders accept the offer, and Greystone will cease to exist.'

'I take it that there's no place for Bryant in this brave new world?'

'None whatsoever.'

'It all sounds a touch unethical,' Holt said, wondering why he cared about ethics any more than his grass-eating friends across the road.

Cartwright joined Holt at the window. 'Peaceful creatures, aren't they?' he said. 'That's why I took this office. But I didn't mean still to be in it sixteen years later.'

'I'd have thought they'd be too messy for you,' Holt said. 'All cowpats and bulging udders.'

Cartwright's face arranged itself into something approaching a smile. 'Nature isn't messy,' he said. 'She designed cows perfectly for the job they do.'

Holt wandered back through the building, out of date as it was built, with its many-storeyed squareness and its stilts. He had never liked the place. He found himself at the end of the corridor, at the imposing double doors to the board room, and let himself in quietly. It was cool in there, with the venetian blinds half closed against the sun. He could hear the rise and fall of Jan's voice as she thought of spurious questions to ask Bryant, and he smiled.

The impression of coolness soon went, and, running a finger round his collar, he opened a window. He looked down on the forecourt, to the main entrance where Warwick had been run over. Had Bryant calmly chatted up European customers while someone did that?

The thought wouldn't go away. But the idea was ridiculous. It was completely ridiculous.

Bryant: too mild-mannered to tell him to go to hell, too polite to turn Jan away? But they were all polite. They were all just ordinary people, watching TV, having a drink at lunchtime, playing bridge. And young Warwick apart, someone had undoubtedly beaten and strangled Alison. Someone had attacked Allsopp with an iron bar. One of these nice, ordinary, polite people killed when it suited.

He allowed his thoughts to dwell on what he would use when

the time came. Similar methods? Nothing sophisticated – bombs and guns were out. They could trace that sort of thing too easily nowadays. When he knew who, he'd know how. And where. Bryant? Living quietly, on his own. He'd be easy. Paranoid, Charles said. Paranoid enough? Enough to arrange to be in Brussels while someone did away with Warwick? He looked again at the forecourt, and smiled. No. It was ridiculous.

Anyway, why take Cartwright's word that he wasn't involved with Alison? Trust no one. Yet he had believed Cartwright, for all that. So maybe Bryant was paranoid. And maybe Wendy was right: Alison hadn't been having an affair at all.

He left the board room, knocked on Bryant's corridor door, and walked in.

'Just finished,' Jan said.

'I timed it just right, then,' he said, with a smiling friendliness that he could see was baffling Bryant, as it was meant to. 'Did you get what you needed?'

'Yes, thank you. Mr Bryant was very helpful.'

'I'll be out in a minute,' he said, and she took her cue like the professional she was, and went through to the secretary's office.

'Thanks, Bob,' he said, still with his golfing-buddy voice. 'It's important to her.'

Bryant frowned. 'I can't imagine why some American magazine is in the least interested in me,' he said.

'Some sort of British week,' Holt said, positively beginning to see the run-down block on the less prosperous side of Milwaukee which doubtless housed the mythical offices of the *Wisconsin Business Digest*, and the has-been reporters who hacked a living there. 'Anything to fill up the pages, I suppose. But it's good money by Jan's standards.'

Bryant nodded. 'She's an attractive girl,' he said.

For just an instant, Holt felt the stab of jealousy that he had felt when Alison had announced that she was going to marry Bryant, then felt foolish. 'So what's she doing with me?' he said lightly.

'Yes, all right,' Bryant said. 'What is she doing with you?'

'She's a friend of mine,' said Holt.

'Was she a prison visitor or something?'

'Sort of. Why, does it matter to you?'

Bryant folded his glasses and put them in his pocket. 'Does she know what you were in there for?' he asked, not looking at him.

For the first time since he got the scar on his arm, Holt felt himself go on the defensive. 'Yes,' he said. 'What have you been saying to her?'

Bryant looked up, surprised. 'Nothing,' he said. 'We were talking about the company.' He pushed his chair back, and stood up. 'But I hope she knows what she's doing.'

'Meaning?'

'She could get hurt,' Bryant said.

Was it a threat? Holt, fresh from imagining Bryant socialising as his young rival was mown down by a lackey, could almost believe that it was. 'And who's going to hurt her?' he asked, his voice low.

'You,' Bryant said. 'One way or the other.'

Jan had made an impression. 'Speaking of people getting hurt,' Holt said. 'You didn't seriously believe it was young Warwick, did you?'

Bryant reacted slightly, but carried on putting folders away in his confidential filing cabinet. So confidential that he had to do his own filing in it. My God, had he *ever* been part of this make-believe world?

'You know about that, do you?' Bryant said. 'Oh, I suppose Alison told you.'

Holt moved quickly to Bryant's side of the desk, and slammed shut the filing cabinet. 'Did it ever occur to you,' he asked, 'that if you had to keep changing your mind about who it was, maybe it wasn't anyone at all?'

'I didn't keep changing my mind,' Bryant said quietly. 'Alison kept changing hers.'

'Alison?' Holt said, uncomprehendingly.

'Alison,' said Bryant.

'You are paranoid.'

'She admitted to them' said Bryant, his voice weary. 'All of them.'

'All of them?' Holt said, bewildered. 'Alison?' The idea shocked him even more than her betrayal of him.

'I don't know why you're so surprised,' Bryant said. 'She rang me up about you.'

Holt didn't believe this was happening to him. Too many questions, too many accusations to give voice to them all. One. Just one. 'You didn't tell the police.'

'Why should I? What I had to tell the police was bad enough, without telling them that she slept with every Tom, Dick and Harry she could find.'

'They were sending me to prison!'

'Because you killed her,' Bryant said. 'That was all that mattered. Really mattered. What difference did it make who else she'd been with? It had no bearing on it.'

The man was a monster. He was looking for a monster, and he'd found him. Now. Here. No, not here. Not now. Later. Later, when he was alone and vulnerable.

'Why did you want Warwick to be at that meeting with Spencer?' he asked. 'The day he died?'

Bryant frowned. 'That's a very rapid change of subject,' he said.

'Is it? Why, Bob?'

'I wanted notes of it.'

'That wasn't Warwick's job.'

'Perhaps I wanted to remind him who was boss,' Bryant said.

Holt took a moment to compose himself, and sat down. 'Why didn't you just sack him?' he asked.

'I couldn't. And he knew I couldn't. If Thelma Warwick had pulled out of Greystone then, we'd have been in trouble.'

Holt searched his pockets for the photograph of Alison. 'Did Allsopp take that?' he demanded, throwing it on the desk.

Bryant picked it up. 'Allsopp?' he said. 'No, of course not. Why would he?'

'Where did you get it?'

'I didn't. The police found it somewhere. They asked if it was a good likeness, and I said yes.'

'And you didn't know where it had come from?'

'Later, I thought you must have taken it. Obviously not.'

Holt's head was swimming. 'And you didn't tell them that you

88

didn't know anything about it? They just thought it was an ordinary photograph?'

'I don't know what they thought! Alison was dead! That was all I was thinking about!'

'You were protecting your pride.'

'No, Alison . . . Oh, I don't know why she did it. Maybe she couldn't help it. But I wasn't dragging her name through the mud.'

'Especially since it was the same as yours?'

'I don't know why I'm even talking to you,' he said. 'There was never any doubt, and there still isn't. So get out. Just get out.'

Holt marshalled his thoughts. 'No,' he said. 'No, you answer me something. After the call — when you went walking to cool off — who did you think she was with?' He banged his fists on the desk. 'Who?'

'I didn't know,' Bryant said. 'I even . . . well, I thought perhaps it was no one. Sometimes . . . sometimes I thought she was making it all up.' He turned away. 'But she wasn't,' he said.

'Why didn't you go home?' Holt asked. 'After she rang you?'

'Do you think I haven't asked myself that?' Bryant said. 'I keep wondering if I'd gone home perhaps I could have stopped it. The doctor said she would have been dead before I got there, but I can't be sure.'

Neither could Holt.

'I don't suppose,' Bryant said haltingly, 'that I gave her much of a life. She said I married Greystone, not her. Perhaps that was true.'

Holt got up slowly. 'Do you believe I killed her?' he asked.

Bryant looked up at him. 'I did,' he said. 'I knew what she could be like.' He looked down at the desk, at the photograph. 'I don't know any more,' he said.

Holt picked up the photograph, and left.

Nine

'Bill,' she pleaded, as she drove back to the hotel. 'Please, Bill, what's wrong?'

He had asked her to drive. He couldn't drive, not with the pain, the crushing pain, where the knot was being pulled so tight that soon it would tear apart in sheer frustration.

She slowed the car down, and pulled into a lay-by.

'Tell me what happened,' she said.

He told her, and she listened, her eyes widening further with each revelation.

'My God,' she said, when he'd finished.

He nodded in silent agreement. My God. It had seemed so easy, in prison, when he'd thought of it. Talk to them. Years later, just talk to them. They'll say things, he had thought. Things they've forgotten. Things they've remembered. Things they didn't say at the time. But my God.

'Who do you believe?' Jan asked.

'Oh, hell. I don't know.' He looked across at her. 'But Alison didn't waste any time with me. Perhaps young Warwick was offered a similar service.'

'So Charles Cartwright is lying when he says he had nothing to do with Alison?' she said.

'Yes,' Holt said, and he was having to blink fast to keep her from seeing the tears of frustration. Tears weren't macho. Tears weren't threatening. Tears were for losers. 'But why? You didn't see him,' he said. 'I believed him.'

'*And* Bryant?'

'All right,' he said, not looking at her, but at the fields and the trees that he had longed to see, and that he couldn't see for the tears in his eyes. Back to square one.

'You were bound to get told different things,' she reminded him. 'You told me you had to collate the information, evaluate it, and compare it with the rest.'

'But I wasn't supposed to believe them all!' He lifted his hands. 'Sorry,' he said. 'I don't know why I'm shouting at you.' He sighed. 'Whoever killed Alison set me up for Allsopp's murder. He had to know that I was with Alison, and neither of them could have known. Unless . . . ' He was unwilling to voice his thought, even now. Even to Jan.

'Unless what?' she said, inevitably.

'Unless Bryant hired someone to do it,' he muttered.

'What?'

'It's possible.'

'It isn't,' she said. 'How? Where would he find someone to do that? Look up assassin in the yellow pages?'

She was ridiculing it. He had known she would. But was it so ridiculous? 'Maybe he already had someone,' he said. 'Cartwright says Alison was in the office when Warwick had his accident. But that was the week that Allsopp was watching her, and there's no mention of her visiting Greystone in his report.'

Jan stared at him. 'What are you saying?' she asked.

'I'm saying that Allsopp was there when Warwick died,' Holt said. 'And he was there when Alison died. That's all.'

'You're saying that he killed them!'

'Maybe.'

Jan looked at him uncertainly. 'You don't really believe all this, do you, Bill?' she said.

'He was there.'

'He wasn't. He was in the pub when Alison died, and if he doesn't mention Greystone, then he probably wasn't there either. Cartwright could be lying.'

'Why? Why would he lie about Alison being there?'

'To give himself an alibi,' said Jan, starting the car crossly. 'To make you think just what you are thinking. To confuse you. I don't know.'

They sat in uncomfortable silence. Holt had expected her to drive off, but she didn't. She was thinking about what he had said, however silly she had said it was.

'And who killed Allsopp?' she said at last.

'Bryant.'

'Why? What would be the point? If he was going to kill

91

anyone, why not kill Alison in the first place?'

'Because who do you think the police suspected in the first place?' he said angrily. 'Bryant was with them for almost two days until he proved he was somewhere else altogether. Because he *was* somewhere else altogether. That was the point.'

And again, they sat in hostile silence. The chocolate-box picture framed in the windscreen would have suited Spencer's competition, Holt thought. Tall trees shifting in the breeze that still helped to cool everything down a little. Swift moving swathes of cloud, lower in the sky than they had been. And bridging the blue expanse between them, an unnatural straight line.

He watched as the thin jet vapour grew wispy and began to break and disappear. Industry and the countryside. Less obvious than the ones Spencer had come up with. Holt might not have done much photography, but how pedestrian could you get? And then he felt it. A little *frisson* of excitement. He'd thought of something valid, but he wasn't sure what.

'Anyway,' Jan said, and the moment was lost. 'If Bryant had hired Allsopp to kill Alison, he'd have made sure he was with someone the whole time, wouldn't he? He'd hardly have gone wandering off on his own. It would have defeated the object.'

Yes. Yes, it would. Holt relaxed a little. 'You're right,' he said.

'Good. Now, Warwick's accident,' she said briskly. 'The *Courier* must have covered it. I'll find out what happened in the end. Did the police ever charge anyone, or what?' She moved out on to the road. 'And if Bryant's telling the truth about Alison,' she said. 'If she had worked her way through Greystone's staff, she might well have moved on to Spencer.'

The competition. There was something about the competition. He tried to recapture it, but it was like trying to remember a dream. He wasn't sure he'd even known what it was before Jan spoke. He was deep in thought as they came into the town, and looked up as they passed the police station. He looked away again.

The inspector sighed. 'Look, son,' he said. 'You've given us one false statement already. They all count against you in court. First

92

you say that Mrs Bryant picked you up at the station, took you home, and drove off with the glasses in the boot of her car . . . ' He paused. 'Then you changed your story – said you went to her house, where you had sex with her.'

Holt nodded. It sounded dreadful, put like that.

'It was in order to conceal this from your wife that you lied.'

Holt nodded.

'You were with her when she made the phone call to her husband?'

'Yes. I've told you everything.'

'Not quite everything,' said the inspector. 'Look, it was a dirty trick. Enough to make anyone lose their temper. So why don't you just write down what happened, and explain why? Explain why you did it.'

'No!' Holt shouted, suddenly galvanised into protest. 'I didn't kill her. I just left. I just — '

But someone had come to the door, and the inspector had gone out. Holt looked at the uniformed policeman who sat in the room with him. 'I didn't kill her,' he said, helplessly.

'Well, well, well,' the inspector said, as he came back in. 'I was wasting my sympathy, wasn't I?'

Holt looked up at him.

'Perhaps you'd like to tell us about this letter,' he said, holding up Allsopp's letter to him.

'Where did you get that?'

'Don't worry, Mr Holt. We had a search warrant. And I sent a couple of my lads out to interview Allsopp, to see what he wanted with you. But they couldn't interview him, could they?'

Oh, God. He'd been going to tell them about the caravan, but they kept asking questions about Alison. One thing at a time, the inspector had said. No hurry. Tell us in your own time. Then just kept asking the same questions about Alison, over and over. He'd been going to tell them.

The inspector waved a hand at him. 'Are these the clothes you were wearing earlier today?'

'Yes,' he said, not really taking in the question. 'Listen, I found the caravan empty. You've got to believe me – it was *empty*.'

93

'Take your clothes off,' the inspector said. 'The constable will bring you something to wear.'

'Take my —'

'Now,' he said, and turned to the other man. 'Tell them I want his fingerprints checked against whatever they find in the caravan,' he said.

Jan got out of the car as soon as they arrived at the George. 'If I go now, I might catch the right person at the paper,' she said. 'I'll find out everything I can . . . and see you back here?'

Holt nodded, bemused still. Jan drove off, and for a few moments he stayed in the passenger seat, trying to make sense of it all. It had never made sense, and now it was even worse. All those things that hadn't been said at the time, and all of them saying that it wouldn't have made any difference. The worst thing of all was that it wouldn't have.

So what if Spencer had known that Bryant had gone missing? So what if he kept quiet about seeing Alison at the station? That would just have got him arrested sooner. And Bryant was right. Telling everyone that Alison was sleeping around would hardly have made matters any easier – it would just have seemed all the more likely that she had driven him to murder.

But someone had done it. Someone had killed her. Someone who knew he'd been with Alison. But who could know that? Only Alison, for God's sake. Only Alison. And Allsopp himself, if his ridiculous theory was right. But it couldn't be. It was preposterous, and the police said Allsopp had been in the pub. So whoever killed her, it wasn't Allsopp.

He sat up, staring into the middle distance as though he could see what had happened if he looked hard enough. Alison *thought* Allsopp was there. She thought she was being watched; when someone started threatening her, wouldn't she use that? Wouldn't she say that someone was watching, to try to stop her attacker? Was *that* how the killer knew about Allsopp?

Spencer. Perhaps he had known Alison. Perhaps that was how come he had picked Greystone when he was looking for a backer. And when he saw her at the station that evening, he went to the house, and realised what was happening. Lost his temper, and attacked her. Did she scream at *him* that Allsopp was watching? That would explain the time delay before Allsopp was killed. Spencer would have to find out who he was, where he lived. Then how to set Holt up.

Holt slid over to the driving seat. Was it Spencer? He drove out of the car park, and out into the narrow street. Had Spencer come to take photographs and visit Thelma, or to see Alison? Was it Bryant? Had he arranged that meeting just so that Warwick would be where he wanted him? Why hadn't Spencer turned up?

Maybe, he thought, heading for Spencer's house, because there never was a meeting.

Jeff Spencer opened the door.

'Bill, come in. Not brought your girl?'

'No,' Holt said. 'I thought . . . ' He looked past Spencer's shoulder. 'Are you alone?' he asked.

'No,' he said. 'But I think Thelma's reconciled to the fact that she has to meet you some time.'

'I'd rather talk in private.'

Spencer smiled. 'That sounds very ominous,' he said. He stood aside to let Holt in. 'I'm British enough to have a front room I never use,' he said, opening the first door off the corridor.

Holt went into a small square room, the walls of which were decorated with black and white photographs.

'Have a seat,' said Spencer. 'Can I get you a drink?'

'No,' Holt said, sitting on an uncomfortable wicker chair. 'Thanks.'

Spencer took the sofa. 'So,' he said. 'What can I do for you?'

'I'm talking to people,' Holt said. 'And they're beginning to tell me things. Nothing important – I mean, everything important was said at the time, wasn't it?'

'I guess,' said Spencer.

'Irrelevancies,' Holt continued. 'Bits and pieces; things that seem quite unimportant, but they could help me. Do you see?'

'I think so,' said Spencer. 'And what bit of irrelevant information do you think I might have?'

Holt regarded him for a moment before speaking. It wasn't going to be easy to catch Spencer off guard. If that was what he

95

intended doing. He didn't know yet.

'Thelma's son,' he said, plunging in at the deep end. 'You were supposed to be at that meeting, weren't you? The day he had his accident?'

'Yes, I was,' Spencer said. 'I'm glad I didn't make it now.'

'Do you remember why you didn't make it?' Holt asked, feeling foolish now that he was actively pursuing his theory.

'Do I,' said Spencer. 'The old girl let me down once too often. Sir Ralph Grey, waiting for me to turn up, and I hadn't even left London.' He smiled. 'That's when I decided to let the train take the strain,' he said.

'I thought it was the cost of petrol,' Holt said.

'That too. And the traffic in London. It wasn't worth trying to keep her on the road. Why do you ask?'

Holt almost blushed. 'Oh, no reason,' he said. 'Just a thought I had. Not worth discussing.'

'Is that all you wanted to know?' Spencer asked.

'No,' said Holt. 'Not quite. Tell me what you know about Alison Bryant.'

Spencer picked up a box of cigars. 'Next to nothing,' he said, flipping open the lid, and offering the box to Holt, who waved it away.

'She was murdered,' Holt said. 'My trial was big news round here. Don't tell me you didn't hear things about Alison.'

'Sure,' said Spencer, selecting a cigar. 'But that was just gossip, hearsay.' He clipped the end, and picked up a table lighter.

'We're not in a court of law,' Holt said. 'I'll admit gossip and hearsay.'

'Nothing,' said Spencer. 'Nothing really. Not about her. People thought that Bob had done it, because the police interviewed him so often. So there were a lot of people who always knew that there was something funny about him, you know. That's all. Nothing, like I said.'

He puffed at the cigar, reminding Holt irresistibly of a movie gangster. 'People said that she'd never been happy with Bob, that sort of thing.' He sat down again. 'During the trial, most people were surprised − shocked, even. About what you said that she had done. I mean, they didn't believe she had initiated it.'

'Most people?' Holt leant forward into a cloud of cigar smoke. 'But not you?'

'Well, Bob and I got quite close after Alison died. He needed someone to talk to, I guess.' He stood up. 'Sure you won't have a drink?'

'Don't let me stop you,' Holt said.

'Thelma fixes the best dry martinis you'll ever taste; it would give you an appetite for dinner.'

'I'm sure she has no desire to fix one for me,' Holt said.

'Maybe you're right,' said Spencer.

'What about Bob? Did he say something?'

The tip of Spencer's cigar glowed. 'Look, Bob was in a bad way. He was drinking a bit more than he should for a while afterwards. He told me things. I don't think I should repeat them.'

'I think you should.' Holt got up from his uncomfortable perch, and strolled to the window.

'But it wouldn't help you,' Spencer said. 'It doesn't make any difference.'

'So everyone says.' Holt turned. 'What did he tell you?'

Spencer laid the cigar in a huge mosaic ashtray. 'All right,' he said. 'Everyone thinks what she did that day was out of character. But I gather that she was, well, more than a little free with her favours.'

Holt's shoulders drooped. Was that it? The big secret? 'Did she ever offer her favours to you?' he asked.

Spencer gave a short sigh. 'I never met the woman,' he said. 'How many more times?' He picked up his cigar. 'I saw her once. That evening, at the station. I didn't even know it was her.'

He jammed the cigar back into his mouth, then took it out again. 'All I knew was that you had some beautiful dame coming up and kissing you. And I wondered when I'd get that lucky.' He shrugged, and laid the cigar down again. 'And from what I've heard, I'd have got lucky sooner than I thought. Except that I wouldn't have been that dumb.' He stood up. 'And what I've just said is between you and me,' he said. 'OK?'

97

'It makes no difference,' Holt said. 'Does it?' He was walking round, looking at the photographs.

Spencer, with fake moustache and Mississippi gambler clothes against a background of dollar bills.

Light, filtered through a window, falling on an empty martini glass with an olive in it, and a woman's stocking lying carelessly beside it.

An old, cobbled alley-way, with back-to-back houses lining it, going on for what seemed like for ever. It could have been 1910, except for the forest of television aerials.

Industry and the countryside wasn't represented. He felt it again, the tremor that meant he was on to something, if only he knew what.

'Are you interested in photography?' asked Spencer.

'Yes,' said Holt. 'Or, at least, I was getting quite interested before they put me away.'

'Couldn't you do that sort of thing in prison? I thought they encouraged hobbies.'

'I didn't want a hobby. I just wanted out.'

'You are out,' Spencer said.

'So?'

'Look, Jan's a nice girl. Why don't you give this up, and just be glad you've met her?'

'I am glad I've met her.'

'Then don't hurt her. Stop raking over the coals.'

Holt's eyes narrowed. 'You're another one? Leave well alone? Just be glad they abolished hanging, and forget that there's a murderer on the loose?'

'I just think you'll do more harm than good. It's over. You're out. You've met someone – settle down with her.'

'And do what? Stand for the council? Join the Freemasons? If I wanted to do that I couldn't, because I'm a murderer.'

'Who says you can't? Look, even if it was wrong, you're free. You've paid your debt to society, and all that.'

'Society hasn't paid its debt to me,' Holt said.

Ten

Everyone liked Jeff Spencer. Holt liked him too. But he realised, on his way back to the George, that so much of Spencer was an act that no one could really trust him. The talk got more New York — more *stage* New York — the more charming he became. Men were all guys, women were all dames, and in full flow he sounded as though he'd walked out of the pages of Damon Runyan. And he was a hustler. Which meant that he'd lie as soon as look at you, and it meant that he'd tell you he was a liar. So you never knew where you were with the man.

In fact, he thought, as he went up to his room after dinner, he had only really known where he was with his fellow inmates. Everyone else had an axe to grind.

'I'll be honest with you, Holt. I can only use the weapons you give me, and you've given me a flintlock pistol to use against a guided missile.'

Holt really needed someone practising *bons mots* on him. 'It's the truth,' he said.

'I don't doubt it,' said the barrister.

Oh, but you do, thought Holt. You do.

'Bill,' said his solicitor. 'There's strong evidence of provocation. Now, if you did do it, you should tell us. Then we can try to —'

'What?' Holt looked from one to the other. 'You think I did it, both of you!'

'No,' said the barrister. 'If you say you didn't do it, then that's what we are bound to believe. And we will defend you to the best of our ability. But I can't pretend it will be easy, in the face of evidence.'

No one. No one would *listen*.

Jan came back, with what information there was on the hit and

99

run. There had been precious little evidence to go on, because no one had actually seen it happen. All the police really knew was that the vehicle was probably a car, and that there wouldn't have been very extensive damage.

'They think there was more than one person in the car,' Jan said. 'They think they had been drinking, and were using the Greystone car park to turn.'

The police were certain that the car hadn't been taken to any of the local garages, and had assumed that it had been from out of town.

'Probably just shot on to the main road,' Jan said. 'Then it could have gone anywhere.'

She had changed out of the skirt and blouse.

'How come Warwick died?' Holt asked. 'If there wasn't much damage to the car?'

A pale green shirt, and the green trousers that he'd seen before. The shirt was cut like a man's, with an old-fashioned shirt-tail. She wore it loose over the trousers.

'They don't really know that it was a car,' she said. 'But the old man says it was.'

'What old man? I thought you said no one saw the accident?'

'He didn't,' she said. Her hair curled on to the collar of the shirt. 'He was blind.'

'Oh?'

'And Warwick was thrown against the concrete gate post,' she said. 'It was the impact with it that killed him. Not impact with the car.'

'So if Allsopp was Bryant's hit-man, he wasn't very good at his job?'

'No.' Jan smiled. 'You don't really believe that, do you?'

She had given him her assessment of Bryant; he was eager to please, courteous, and he didn't invite her to have a spot of lunch with him. Bryant had never married again; Jan hadn't known that, and when Holt told her, she had looked thoughtful, then said, 'No. I don't suppose he did.'

'Why?' he had asked.

'Because a wife would be a nuisance,' she had said. 'She would come between him and Greystone.'

Holt had asked her to expand, and she had said she couldn't. It was just that she had never heard 'I' so much in one conversation. Not even Ralph Grey had taken such a personal view of Greystone. He said 'we' or 'Greystone'. Bryant said 'I'.

I, Bryant. Egomania? It didn't usually result in multiple murder. But all that prison psychology which he had thought would help him, was no help at all.

He had seen murderers. He had watched them, he knew what they were like. But they were the bad guys, the crooks, the thugs. The men who carried guns or knives or knuckle-dusters. He had come to know them, and to understand them, and often to like them. To them, violence was just an occupational hazard, like prison. They killed one another; the law was an interference they could do without. They had their own laws.

And one of those laws was that you didn't kill innocent young women, and his ride in prison was the rougher for it, until he got tough himself. But none of that helped now. Because how could you spot which of these middle-class sober citizens just deliberately destroyed people who got in his way? One of these people was ruthless and violent. One of them was capable of anything.

'I wish I could have spoken to the old man,' he said.

'Why?'

'There was a blind man in prison. George. George knew more about what was going on than the rest of us put together.'

Jan began looking through her notes.

'If you wanted to know if a screw was coming, you asked George. If you wanted to know *which* screw was coming, you asked George.'

She smiled. 'Well,' she said. 'The *Courier* didn't know much about him; they only found out where he lived after the accident had stopped really being news any more. So he was just a note on the file. And he doesn't live at that address now. I checked.'

'So he'll have to stay just a note on the file,' Holt said.

'No!' she said vehemently. 'I'll find him.'

Holt sighed. 'How are you going to find him? He's probably dead by now.'

'I'll find him,' she said firmly, and stood up. 'You shouldn't be cooped up in here,' she said. 'Let's go for a walk.'

He wasn't enthusiastic, but if she wanted to walk, they would walk.

The traffic fumes that filled the air of the pedestrian precinct during the day were gone from the quiet night-time streets, and Holt breathed in the peace and quiet. They weren't walking anywhere in particular; just past shops, some that he remembered from boyhood, some that he'd never have believed. A sex shop, with its windows painted, like the doctor's surgery used to be. A side street beckoned, looking as it always had. He turned down it, and Jan followed.

'But Cartwright couldn't have got to the Bryants' house and back in time,' Jan said, obviously carrying on an argument with herself. 'Could he?'

Half an hour. No, thought Holt. The police said Bryant couldn't have done it, so neither could Cartwright. But maybe, if he really put his foot down. If, if, if. No. No, he couldn't have.

They had got to the park, but the gates were closed. Jan pushed them hopefully, but they were locked. In the moonlight, it looked mysterious and a little sad. Not like the place where the children played at all. A huge lorry roared past, the tail wind catching them, making Jan's shirt cling to her. 'Where now?' she asked, when the noise died away.

Holt looked round at the empty street. 'We walk back, I suppose,' he said.

She came up to get her briefcase.

'What are you living on?' Holt asked, suddenly aware for the first time that she had taken him on as a full-time job.

'I'm all right,' she said.

'But you're not doing any proper work,' he insisted.

'This is more important,' she said.

'Well, if you needed money, you would tell me, wouldn't you?'

'Yes,' she said, with smiling directness.

'Good.'

She picked up her notebook. 'I'll find out who lives at this address now,' she said. 'See if I can trace the old man.' She popped the notebook in her briefcase, and turned to him. 'Allsopp wasn't good at his job, was he?' she said. 'According to him Alison only ever saw Cassie and your wife. And she stayed at home the rest of the time.'

'Wendy says that's how it was.'

Jan nodded. 'Can I take the reports?' she asked, reaching across him to the bedside table. A faint perfume, a brush of her body against his. It wasn't a calculated move; it wasn't another of her attempts to turn him on. But she did.

He moved away.

'You don't want to get locked out again,' he said, opening the door.

'No,' she agreed, and locked her briefcase. She stopped as she was leaving. 'You should let go,' she said, kissing him on the cheek. Then she was gone, her feet hurrying away down the stairs.

Holt went down after a few moments, and bought some whisky. He had made quite a mark on it by the time he lay down on the bed, and snapped off the light.

The night had grown oppressively hot once more, and Holt smoked in the darkness, trying to make some sense of it all. He felt as though he were slipping in and out of some alternative universe where everything looked the same, but it wasn't. Allsopp was there, Allsopp wasn't there. Alison was promiscuous, Alison was practically a born-again virgin. Bryant was a maniac, Bryant was a martyr. Cartwright was a victim, Cartwright was a vicious killer.

Allsopp *was* Bryant's hit man. Not very good; that would be about right. Scraped a win over Warwick, and dispatched Alison with more efficiency. Then Bryant got worried, and did away with Allsopp. This unlikely image of Bryant still made him smile, and he couldn't take it seriously.

Spencer had been having an affair with Alison, saw them together, and killed her in a rage. She had said that someone was watching, and Bryant, looking for a shoulder to cry on, had confided in him about Allsopp. So then he killed Allsopp.

Cartwright might have overheard what Alison had said on the phone to Bryant; you could sometimes hear what people on the other end were saying. So he had rushed over there, and killed her. Allsopp, doing his detective work, had found out too much, and Cartwright had killed him too. Except that Cartwright was on a train at the time.

He smiled, remembering the magic train. Where would he take it? To another country, another planet? Back to 1970, like he'd said? No. Before then. Before his life crumbled. But then he would never have met Jan. And he didn't think he would want to be back in a world without Jan. To the future then, somewhere sunny and warm, so that Jan would stay brown.

He had to be careful now. Very careful. Whoever did it didn't hesitate to kill, as the judge had so rightly said to the wrong man. Jan was in too deep to avoid the danger, and he had to tread warily. He mustn't let the murderer get scared. And if that did happen, then he must be ready to push Jan one way and himself the other.

He wanted it to be morning. He wanted to hear her knock, to see her face, to watch her move and see what she was wearing. He wanted just to listen to her, to smell her freshness, after so many years of masculinity. Her enthusiasm, her sparkle. That was all he needed from her, all he wanted.

He poured himself another drink, noticing the drop in the level. What the hell? He was his own man again. If he wanted to get drunk all alone in the middle of the night in a hotel room, that was his privilege. No more loss of privileges.

She must only have been eighteen when she came to see him on the roof. She had stood out there, in that freezing weather, and that brought a lump to his throat.

The roof. Clinging to a roof, shouting that he hadn't killed anyone. That was how Jan had described him.

Someone killed Alison. Someone wanted Alison Bryant dead badly enough to kill her, even though Alison must have said that someone was watching. She would have shouted, screamed for help. Who would have wanted her dead that badly? One of her lovers?

Allsopp hadn't found out anything about her lovers. As Jan had said: if Alison was so active, wouldn't even Allsopp have heard some gossip? And that puzzled him more than anything, for Alison's sex life was something to which he had never given a thought until he was briefly part of it.

She *wasn't* someone people gossiped about, or someone men nudged one another about. She was quite beautiful; that wasn't the same thing.

Until that day, he had never had waves from Alison, not even when they were supposedly courting, in their teens. She'd kissed him goodnight and all that, but even then it hadn't been particularly exciting, because she hadn't wanted it to be, until that day, when she had put her heart and soul into it. Though he doubted now if she had had a heart or a soul.

But for this whole business to hinge on Alison's sex appeal seemed very odd to him; she really hadn't been that kind of a girl. And even that day, if he forced himself to think about it, she had only gone through the motions. Once she'd landed him, so to speak, she had more or less abdicated. He had put it down to her eagerness to make her wicked phone call, but now he thought that it was just as he would have expected; Alison wasn't terribly interested in him, and never had been. In any man, really.

He couldn't believe that it had taken him this long to realise that; it had been staring him in the face since she was fifteen years old.

Eleven

'Listen,' she was saying, before he'd got the door open properly. 'I've —'

He put a finger to his lips, and she stopped speaking. He didn't think he could take her enthusiasm right now. He had finally slept as dawn had begun to invade his dark, hot privacy, and had been awakened by Jan's knock. His head ached, his tongue was dry, and he was in his underpants. Very natty wine-coloured underpants which matched a vest that it was too hot to wear, but underpants for all that.

'Not so loud,' he said, in a voice thick with hungover sleep. Talking seemed a bit dangerous. He might throw up if he had to do too much of it. He walked towards the bathroom, trying to keep his head very still. 'I'll . . . ' He made shaving motions. 'Order coffee,' he managed to croak, waving towards the phone.

He stared at the electric shaver, and weighed up the pros and cons. Electric shavers made a dreadful noise. Razors were no fun when your hand was shaking. He decided, and shaved while the water ran into the bath, to get both noises over at once. It was almost worth it for the indescribable relief when it stopped. The bath helped slightly, and he went back out briefly, wearing the new bath-robe that had cost so much he almost hadn't bought it.

Jan was making the bed; she opened her mouth, but he held up a hand. 'Wait,' he said, selecting clothes with less care than usual, and he went back to the silent sanctuary of the bathroom.

Dressed, he felt less vulnerable, and his head seemed still to be on his shoulders. He opened the bathroom door as the coffee arrived, and Jan took up her customary position on the bed, bare legs tucked under her. She opened the briefcase, and started surrounding herself with papers.

Holt swallowed some coffee, and looked at her through eyelids that still weren't too keen to open properly. 'I tied one on,' he said. 'As your friends in Wisconsin would say.'

'Did it help?'

'No.'

Her sandals, kicked off as usual, lay by his feet. He smiled at her. She never wore jewellery: no studs in her ears, no chains round her neck. No bracelets, not even a watch. He hadn't realised that before. 'Hello,' he said.

'Hello.'

'What kind of school did you go to?' he asked.

'Comprehensive.'

That was one of the things he loved about Jan. She asked questions – my God, did she ask questions. But she lived and died by the sword, and she answered them too, without asking for reasons.

'I went to a boarding school,' he said. 'All male.'

She frowned very slightly, then looked enquiringly at him.

'In boys' schools,' he went on, 'there's always a possibility of homosexuality – like in prison,' he added.

She looked at him thoughtfully. 'I hope you're not trying to tell me something,' she said.

'What?' he said, puzzled. Then his brow cleared. 'Oh,' he said. 'No.'

'Good.'

He drank some coffee. 'Do you think it's the same in girls' schools?' he asked.

'Well,' she said, leaning back, her elbow on the pillow, her head on her hand. 'They don't get so hot under the collar about it, do they? They just call them crushes and get on with their lives.'

'Do you think a crush could last? Long enough to blossom again ten years later?'

Jan looked at him seriously for a moment. 'Alison and Cassie?' she said. The question mark was there, but she was nodding slowly as she spoke.

'It makes more sense than anything else,' Holt said. 'You said yourself that Cassie's mentioned all the time in Allsopp's reports.'

He moved over as she took the reports from her briefcase, and sat beside her on the bed. It was the first time he had voluntarily got close to her, and he knew that she had noticed. He looked over her shoulder at the reports. 'See?' he said. 'I think that's what Allsopp realised.'

She folded up the reports. 'Cassie?' she said quietly.

Holt had faced it in the small hours. Somehow the thought that it might have been Cassie had momentarily wiped the shine off his plan. But if it was Cassie, then it was, and no one had the right to send a man to prison for a third of his life. No one. If it was Cassie who did that to him, then she had better look over her shoulder in dark alleys.

'Don't worry,' Jan said. 'There are other contenders.'

Worry? He wasn't worrying. He was planning.

'I've found him,' she said.

'Who?' Holt asked, puzzled.

'The old man. Mr Denton.' She looked triumphant. 'It took me less than a morning. I rang the people at his old address, and they said they'd bought the house from someone called Reynolds. It was the fourth Reynolds I tried, and she said that the old man sold the house to them when his wife died. So I thought that an old blind man on his own would probably move into a home. I rang round the old people's homes, and this is it.'

She beamed, and held out a piece of paper. 'Do I get a kiss?' she asked.

'What did you *tell* these people?' he demanded, ignoring her.

'Which ones? I told the first ones that I was a temp at the DHSS and I'd made a cock-up on the computer, and I told the Reynolds people that the first lot suggested I ring them, and that did the trick by itself. They didn't want a reason. I told the old people's home that I was doing an article on how people live with physical disabilities.'

'And they all believed you?'

'Why not?'

'Where did you do all this phoning? Your digs? Did your landlady overhear you?'

'Of course not! I rang from a call box.'

'What about the pips? How could you say you were at the DHSS with the bloody pips going?' She'd get him locked up before he'd done anything.

'That box doesn't have pips,' she said, earnestly shaking her head as she spoke.

'What box?'

'The one outside the post office — any of the new ones.'

'New ones?' he repeated.

'Yes,' she said, looking a little uncomfortable. 'They've got blue receivers, and keypads instead of dials.'

He'd seen them. He hadn't used one; that was something else he never wanted to do again.

'Mr Denton might be able to tell us who was there,' she said. 'Maybe Cartwright's lying about Alison.'

But why would Cartwright lie about that?' Holt said, exasperated.

'I don't know,' said Jan, and handed him Allsopp's reports, tapping the entry for 21st March. 'But someone's lying,' she said.

He took the report, and sat without moving for a moment, before screwing it up into a tight ball and hurling it as far as he could across the room.

'All I know,' he said, 'is that I knew Alison all her life. I knew her maybe as well as you can know anyone, because children are honest. They cry if they're hurt, and laugh if they're happy.' He stood up, and reached for his jacket. 'And what I know about Alison simply doesn't fit this . . . this bed-hopping image that Bryant's conjured up!' He threw open the door. 'I'm going to see Cassie.'

He drove to Greystone, the knot in his stomach pulling, straining, trying to free itself. Not yet, he thought, as he strode into the building. Not yet.

He went through the outer office, and into Cassie's, without speaking to the secretary, without knocking. Cassie had someone with her.

'I want to talk to you,' he said, interrupting her visitor.

Cassie looked up at him. Outside, clouds began to gather and the sun dimmed, but the heat was still there; his shirt was sticking to his back.

'Could we come back to this?' she asked the young man with her.

He looked round at Holt. 'Sorry,' he said, as though he were the one who had interrupted, and stood up.

Cassie looked crisp and efficient. Her office was spartan and neat; she didn't surround herself with the clutter of her home, or with beautiful things, like Charles. Just what she needed. Phone, diary, desk, chairs. She must have to switch herself on and off like a light bulb.

'I'll come back, shall I?' the young man asked hesitantly.

'I'll give you a ring,' she said.

The young man smiled nervously at Holt, and went.

Cassie looked up at him, and he placed the photograph of Alison on the desk. Her eyes were sad as she picked it up.

'I've found the right questions,' he said.

She nodded.

'When did it start, Cassie?'

'When she was fifteen and I was seventeen,' she said. 'That's when it started.'

'I'm not talking about a schoolgirl crush,' he said, sitting down.

'Neither am I.' She looked down then, at the blotter on her desk, every inch of which was covered with notes and doodles, the only indication of what Cassie was really like. 'You don't know what we went through,' she said.

'I don't want to know.'

'No,' she said. 'I don't suppose you do. It must be nice knowing that all your hormones are in the right place.'

'I don't give a damn what your preferences are! You let me go to jail.'

Cassie looked shocked. 'I couldn't have stopped that!' she cried. 'Please listen. Try to understand.'

Holt buried his face in his hands, and nodded.

'It was 1956,' she said. 'There wasn't a nice neat word to cover it then, or if there was we didn't know it. We didn't even know if we were breaking the law.'

Holt let his hands slide down his face, and looked over at Cassie.

'We were different,' she went on. 'And frightened. It wasn't like now. It wasn't something you put on badges and tee-shirts.'

'I'm not talking about 1956,' he said wearily.

'I know. But that's when it started, and that's what you asked.

110

We knew how we felt,' she said. 'We tried to ignore it; and in the holidays, we'd come home, and Alison would go dancing with you because she was expected to.' She picked up a pen, and tapped it on the blotter.

'In the end,' she said, 'I accepted it. I wanted Alison to accept it too, but she couldn't. She was ashamed of how she felt.' She looked up at him. 'There were pressures,' she said, drawing slow circles with the cap of the pen in the blotter, making it bite into the paper. 'She was expected to marry, have children; she was expected to marry you.' She got up. 'Why didn't she?' she asked, looking out.

'I never asked her.'

'Why not?'

'Because . . . ' He thought about it. He had always been very fond of Alison, enjoyed being with her. And he had always assumed that he would marry her one day. When they were older. Until he had met Wendy, and realised that there was more to even an innocent relationship than Alison was offering. 'Because I didn't get any encouragement,' he said.

'I don't think Bob ever did either,' she said. 'But he asked her, and she accepted, because she wanted to be "normal".' She gave a little laugh. 'They were a joke, weren't they, those women? You saw them in films: the one who always wore trousers, and the one who was pretty and feminine.' She turned back. 'It wasn't *like* that!' she said, fiercely, quietly. 'We were both women, we were both feminine. Alison couldn't accept it.' She sat down. 'Then I was transferred to London, and she married Bob.'

'Why didn't you stay away?'

Cassie looked up at him. 'Grandfather died,' she said. 'I wanted to come back. I thought I could handle it. Ralph didn't.'

'Ralph *knew*?'

'Oh, he never said he knew in so many words. But he tried to get Alison to change schools. And he packed me off to the London office as soon as I graduated. And then fought like hell to stop me coming back.'

Holt sat back. 'So that's why he suddenly got male chauvinist,' he said. 'But you thought you could handle it.'

'Yes. And perhaps,' she said, 'perhaps if Alison had been

111

happy it would have been all right. But she wasn't. She was miserable. Bob treated her like some sort of domestic appliance that he could unplug when he wasn't using it.' She shook her head. 'I really believe she could have made a go of it if she had had someone who really cared about her,' she said.

'Why did she stay with him?'

'She was going to leave. Years before. But he begged her not to, and she thought she owed him that much.' Cassie etched circles in the blotter as she spoke. 'She gave him far more than she ever got in return,' she said. 'It wasn't her fault that it didn't work, but she thought that it was. She was lonely, and very unhappy, and I couldn't . . . ' She broke off. 'I couldn't handle it.'

She looked again at the photograph. 'She was happy then,' she said. 'For a while. But she still wouldn't leave him. She was still ashamed of us, afraid people would find out. She needed marriage as a sort of cover, I suppose.'

He had been on *trial*. And Cassie hadn't said a word. Not one word.

'You didn't tell anyone,' he said. 'Everyone thought it was me she'd been seeing. And you didn't tell them it wasn't.'

'I couldn't,' she said. 'I *couldn't*. I couldn't do that to her.'

He was getting too angry. He mustn't get angry, not yet. The anger had to wait until the right time and the right place. 'Alison was dead,' he said through his teeth.

'Even so.'

It was growing dark, almost like evening, with the lowering thunderclouds obscuring the sun. Cassie got up and switched on the lights, which flickered, then steadied into a harsh light, and Cassie looked older.

'It didn't alter what had happened,' she said, as she sat down and picked up her pen again. 'It didn't alter what she had done.'

'Why?' he asked, hearing his voice straining to be calm. 'Why did Alison do that to me?'

'You were a decoy,' she said. 'I suppose.'

'What?'

'Bob knew something was going on. He suddenly got jealous, accusing every man she ever so much as nodded to. And she let him jump to whatever conclusion he chose; anything sooner than

112

have anyone know the truth. But he didn't really believe her.'

He'd said that. Bryant had said that.

'So,' Cassie continued. 'When she thought someone was watching her — and you were *there* — she decided to give him some proof. Proof that you couldn't deny.'

If she was expecting him to say something, he couldn't.

'I didn't know what she was going to do,' Cassie said. 'Please believe me. I'd have tried to stop her.'

He was barely listening, until she said that.

'Tried to stop her?' he said, almost whispering, hardly able to speak at all for the knot in his stomach, as it pulled tighter, tighter. 'What do you mean, you'd have tried to stop her?'

'When she rang me,' Cassie said carefully, never taking her eyes from his.

'When?' he roared, jumping up. 'When did she ring you?'

'At about six o'clock,' Cassie said. 'She rang me at home, and said that you were with her, and she was going to tell you about it.'

'Jesus Christ,' he said, sinking back down on to the chair.

Cassie knew he was there. She knew. He had said it had to be someone who knew he was there. The right time, the right place. Then he could let the anger explode in her face like a hand grenade. Not now.

'She said she would see if you could help. Then she suddenly said someone was watching her. He'd been following her, she said. And she hung up.'

At home. She said that Alison rang her at home. So it couldn't have been . . . Cassie's words played in his head, like a tape. *See if you could help.* 'Help?' he said. 'How the hell could I help?'

'Oh, Alison thought men were cleverer than she was,' Cassie said, her voice brittle.

'Cleverer?' he said, confused and angry. 'What about?'

Cassie's eyes widened. 'But I thought you knew, I thought you realised. I thought that was why you showed me the photo.'

He blinked at her.

'Allsopp was blackmailing us, Bill. I thought you knew.'

Holt couldn't speak.

'It began the week Bob was away. Alison paid him off, and we thought that was that, but . . . ' She picked up the photograph.

113

'Alison got this in the post that Friday morning. And a phone call telling her that there were more interesting ones she could buy.'

'What the hell were you doing where he could take photographs of you?' Holt asked.

'You don't have to do much,' she said bitterly. She held out the photograph. 'These dark things at the front. They're the railings on the high-rise opposite my house.' She looked at him. 'He was looking in my window,' she said with a shiver.

The high-rise, and a telephoto lens, and Cassie's high hedges were no protection.

'She went there that afternoon, and paid him money, but he didn't give her the photographs. If there were any. When she got back, she came to see me at the office. Then I got called back into the board room. Alison was in Bob's office, but when I came out, she'd gone.'

Gone to pick him up at the station. Holt felt numb, and the words were washing over him, going into some sort of storage where he could examine them later. Right now, he couldn't cope with them.

'Then she rang me, and said she was going to ask your advice. And you know the rest.'

He knew the rest. He could see pale reflections in the glass, against the blue-black mass of cloud. The back of Cassie's head, her long blonde hair untidy at the back, where she forgot about it. He could see himself, see his own uncomprehending face. In the glass, the room, neat and bare, looked like a prison cell.

Cassie was at home. *At home.* It couldn't have been Cassie. But Allsopp was there, whatever the police thought. 'You knew,' he said. 'You knew Allsopp was there.'

'But it wasn't Allsopp,' she said. 'What would have been the point, if it had been Allsopp? She thought Bob had put another detective on to her. Someone who would really report to Bob. So she gave him something *to* report. Something she could live with.'

The man in the glass looked defeated as she spoke again.

'And,' she said, her voice shaking, 'she pushed you too far. You killed her. *You* killed her. So now you've found out what you wanted to know, just go away. Please just go away.'

114

Twelve

'Remember it?' he said, shouting slightly as the hard of hearing do. 'I'll never forget it. Never.'

Holt, much against his will, was posing as the photographer for an even more obscure journal than the *Wisconsin Business Digest*.

He had gone back to the hotel from Cassie's, bemused and confused, to find the camera, and a note from Jan.

Seeing Mr Denton tomorrow. Thought you might like to take up photography again. Be careful with the camera — it's the Courier's. *Love, Jan.*

He hadn't left his room again. He had stared at the evidence, at the facts, and tried to make sense of it all. But it made no sense.

'Just call me Jan,' she was saying, when the old man asked her name, and her raised voice brought Holt back to the present. This article, she had told Mr Denton, might never actually get into print. But the editor of the Millfield Insurance in-house magazine *Premium*, accommodating chap that he was, had said she could do the interview, and see how it worked out. And it was interesting, after all, that a blind man should be the only witness to a fatal accident.

'So what happened, as far as you were concerned?' she enunciated clearly.

'I heard the car coming, too fast. Then I heard it turn, and then it hit someone. Young lad, he was.'

'What did you do?'

The old man inclined his head towards her, frowning slightly. He was eighty-six, and may have lost one of his faculties and be having trouble with another, but the rest of them were all there.

'I said, what did you do?' she repeated, in clear carrying tones that caused several grey heads to turn, and made Holt feel more foolish than ever. He took a snap of Mr Denton.

115

They were in the grounds of the home, and the residents were making the most of the warm weather, even if the sun was still being shy.

'I went towards the car, and I heard someone get out of the passenger side,' he said. 'But they must have seen the stick, because he just got back in, and the car drove off.'

'He?' Jan said.

'Oh, yes. A man's footsteps. After a good lunch, I'd say. Brandy and cigars.'

'So you don't think it was kids on a joy-ride?' asked Jan.

'What's that?'

Several people were now finding that their strolls were taking them closer to the group by the patio window. Inside, lunch was being prepared, and people were getting the tables ready. Holt took more photos of Mr Denton.

'I said, you don't think it was youngsters?'

'Definitely not,' he said. 'What's all this about, anyway?'

'Well,' said Jan. 'I'm just trying to get background.'

'You're up to something,' he said. 'I'll tell your dad.' And he laughed. 'You're Barney Wentworth's lass. You've forgotten me, haven't you?'

Holt peered into the camera, and if the film was in properly, and if he'd not made too much of a mess of the settings, and if he had pressed the button just when he hoped he had, then he had caught a look on Jan's face that he would treasure.

'I had the shop next door to yours,' he said. 'I've known your mum and dad since they were younger than you. You've got your mum's voice. And you haven't changed. That trick of saying "well" before you thought up some excuse. It always meant devilment.'

'I don't remember you,' she said. 'I'm sorry.'

'You would be about seven when I retired,' he said. 'Is it some sort of devilment?'

'Some sort,' she said. 'Someone's told me they think Roger Warwick was run over deliberately.'

'Never!' he said firmly. 'I've never tried it myself, but if you wanted to run someone over you'd drive the car at them, wouldn't you? Stands to reason.'

116

'Yes.'

'That car swerved, and braked, and its horn was going – that wasn't deliberate. You take my word.'

'I will,' Jan said. 'I don't suppose one of them called the other by name, or anything?'

'No,' he said scornfully. 'I'd have told the police. No,' he said again. 'Funny thing. They didn't speak at all.'

'After they drove off, did you stay?'

'I went to phone the ambulance,' he said. 'Then I went back to him.'

Jan looked across at Holt before she asked the next question. The one the police hadn't known to ask.

'Was there anyone else there?' she asked.

'What's that?'

'Was there anyone else? With the boy?'

'Oh. Not then. But some people came out of the Greystone building – they knew him. He worked there. He'd been with them not ten minutes before.'

'Was there a woman with them?' Jan asked.

'A girl,' he said. 'She was upset – she didn't stay. Her father took her away. The young man stayed though. He dealt with the police and all that.'

He sat back. 'Is that it?' he said. 'What you really wanted to know?'

'Yes,' said Jan, blushing slightly.

Holt smiled. The old man hadn't let him down. But Cartwright was telling the truth; so what the hell was Allsopp doing? Just being bad at his job, according to Mr Harmer. Not running anyone over, according to Mr Denton.

'Barney Wentworth,' Mr Denton said. 'It's a long time since we were together. How is he – how's your mum?'

'They're fine,' said Jan. 'They moved away a few years ago. To the seaside.'

'Your mum always wanted to live by the sea. Sussex, isn't it? She's a nice lass, your mum. You take after her.'

'I must,' she said, smiling.

Mr Denton looked in his direction. 'And why are you here, then?' he asked, with a grin.

117

'Verisimilitude,' said Holt.

It went down very well, and they left him chuckling to himself when they went.

'I warned you,' he said, as Jan got into the car beside him, and let out a sigh, closing her eyes.

'I think I'll put the film in to be developed,' she said. 'Send a photo of him to mum and dad.'

'Is that where you live?' he asked. 'Sussex?'

'Oh, no. I never did live there,' she said. 'I still live in Leeds; that's where the paper was that I worked for.' She smiled. 'I wish I'd brought more clothes with me,' she said. 'Mrs Buxton charges me for the washing machine.' She sat up. 'My parents moved away about ten years ago,' she said, starting the car.

Of course. He still found it difficult to adjust to his lost sixteen years. He thought everyone's life stopped in 1970, and only started again three weeks ago. Jan would be living her own life when her parents moved away.

Holt rubbed his eyes tiredly. Cartwright had been telling the truth, and Allsopp hadn't. Why not? A visit to Greystone wasn't something he was being paid to keep quiet about.

'What was Allsopp up to?' he asked.

Jan shook her head. 'I still don't believe he was mowing Warwick down,' she said, setting off. After a few moments, she snapped her fingers ineffectually, causing the car to swerve rather close to a cyclist. 'We're forgetting Allsopp's hobby,' she said. 'If he saw a hit and run, what do you suppose he'd do?'

'See what was in it for him,' Holt said.

'And leave all mention of Greystone out of his report,' Jan pointed out. 'No wonder he left the agency. He must have been coining it in by then.'

'Left a lot of money, considering,' Holt said, in Harmer's accent.

Jan joined the line of traffic at the lights. 'Well at least that disposes of the assassin theory,' she said. 'I suppose he was going to blackmail you, if someone hadn't got to him first.'

'But how?' said Holt. 'He wasn't there. And he certainly wasn't doing any private investigation. He was annoyed when

118

Alison died, like Harmer said. Annoyed because his source of income had been removed.'

'You've only got Cassie's word for that,' Jan said.

Holt was jolted forward a little as she pulled the car up again as the line stopped moving. 'She'd hardly make it all up,' he said.

'Why not?' Jan asked. 'Someone's making something up.'

She was right. His desire to believe what Cassie had said had its roots in his childhood. Jan didn't have such obstacles to logical thought. He glanced at her, at the white jeans and the pink top, cool and fresh in this oppressive heat. Her face was sad and angry, and he wondered why she cared.

They shunted up the road towards the lights, but they changed again.

'But I believe her,' he said, simply.

'And you believed Cartwright, and you believed Bryant.'

Holt sighed. 'Maybe they're all telling the truth,' he said.

'Perhaps they are,' Jan said, putting the car in neutral and turning to face him, looking serious.

'But they can't all be,' said Holt.

She nodded. 'They can be,' she said. 'because they aren't the only people involved.' She seemed reluctant to go on, and the car horns behind suggested that she should stop talking and start driving, and she did. The lights stayed green for fifteen seconds, and they were stationary again.

'Spencer?' said Holt.

She looked upset, and didn't speak.

'He had no reason to kill Alison,' Holt argued.

Jan moved forward, and at last was free of the lights. After a moment, she spoke again. 'Spencer?' she said lightly. 'Yes, perhaps. Perhaps he did know Alison.'

'But we've been through all that. And Alison wasn't interested in men anyway.'

'She used them, though,' said Jan. 'She didn't mind letting Bryant jump to conclusions, according to Cassie. And she used you. Why not Spencer?' She warmed to her theme. 'If she had, she'd want Bryant to know all about it, wouldn't she? To put him off the scent, as Cassie pointed out.'

The next set of traffic lights loomed, and she slowed down behind a van. Holt wound down the window for some air, but the still, hot day had only exhaust fumes to offer, and he wound it up again.

'And Spencer would have been ruined if Greystone had pulled out of the deal,' she said, the sadness gone, replaced by her old sparkle.

'It's as crazy as all our other theories,' Holt said sourly.

'Someone killed her,' Jan said. 'And you don't believe all that about a photographic competition. Why didn't he go straight to Thelma's? Who says he was taking photographs? Cartwright didn't – he just said he saw him.'

The photographs. Again Holt felt the little flash of knowledge. The photographs were important.

'And maybe Allsopp was watching,' Jan said. 'Despite what everyone says. He could have seen Spencer, and made some enquiries with a view to blackmailing him, for all we know.'

'But it wasn't Allsopp,' Holt said wearily. 'The police say it wasn't. Bryant says it wasn't. Cassie says it wasn't.'

The car jerked its way towards the lights.

'Then who the hell was it?' Jan asked, suddenly sounding as desperate as he felt.

Holt stared at her, then at the camera in the back seat. 'Of course,' he said. 'Of course.'

'What? What is it?'

Damn it, he'd remembered it. Thought about it. And it still hadn't clicked. Every time he'd thought about the photographs, he'd known. And Jan had taken the bloody keys back. They couldn't get them again, not now. It would be too obvious. They'd start asking questions, and it would lead the police to him. He had to be careful that nothing looked odd. No loose ends for people to worry about.

'How do you feel about a spot of house-breaking?' he asked.

'Whose house?' asked Jan.

'The Bryants' old house.'

Jan stopped at the lights. 'No need,' she said, going into her bag and producing shiny new keys. 'I had them copied.' She smiled. 'Do I get a kiss?'

He kissed her on the forehead, and took the keys. 'Let's go,' he said.

Jan thankfully escaped down a side street and back on to the dual carriageway, which swept past all the villages, and took you into Leicester in almost half the time. Took you to Gartree in less than an hour. Off the dual carriageway on to the old road, down into the valley. Turn off as the road starts rising again, and after a moment, you could see the Bryants' house. Going back once had been hell, but this was even worse. Because if he was right, then there was nothing more to do.

He unlocked the door. 'You'll have to be here on your own for a few minutes,' he said. 'Do you mind?'

'No,' she said, following him into the sitting room. 'Was it a nice house?' she asked. 'Was it comfortable?'

Holt tried to see the room as it had once looked. Not as it did now, with bare floor boards and peeling walls; not as he remembered it, with its connotations. As it had looked the first time he saw it, when he and Wendy had come to the house-warming, and he had tried to joke his way through an evening heavy with atmosphere. No, the Bryants had not been happy. And it hadn't been a happy house. 'It had comfortable furniture,' he said. 'Not much else.'

He turned to look at her, and the empty, abandoned house looked more welcoming, now, with Jan in it, than it ever had before. 'It wasn't the house's fault,' he said.

'What do you want me to do?' she asked.

'It'll sound ridiculous,' he said. 'But it's important.'

She smiled. 'It can't sound any more ridiculous than some of the things we've been saying,' she said.

'I'd like you to wait until you hear the car leave, then do what Alison did. Come in here, go into the kitchen, put the kettle on – you know.'

She nodded.

'Then go upstairs, and stand by the writing desk. Look out of the window, and just tell me what you see, and how long it is before you see it.' He smiled. 'If that makes any sense,' he added. 'Use this.' He took off his watch and handed it to her.

'Right,' she said.

121

She hadn't asked what she was doing all this for. She was just doing it.

'I'll go, then,' he said. 'Be careful on the stairs.'

He walked quickly to Jan's car, and got in, taking a deep breath. This would prove or disprove more than one story. He looked back at the house for a moment, then drove off along the road, up the incline, and round the crest of the hill. He had thought he might not see it, but he could just glimpse it through the trees. So he pulled the car off the road there, and reached in for the camera.

He walked along the grassy slope, looking at the valley gently falling away from him. He was concentrating on what he was looking for; he hadn't looked behind him. He didn't know whether you could see the house or not. He wouldn't have known it was there. Not much of a view now, he thought, as he looked through the viewfinder. The bank of trees had been planted to mask it, but sixteen years ago, they were young, slender saplings, and they wouldn't have hidden it then. Trees sometimes did change, he thought, remembering what Jan had said in the wood near Allsopp's place.

He even took a photograph. Maybe it would win a competition.

It was like one of these logic problems that he had done to distraction in prison. You ticked off what you had established, in little boxes, and eventually you were left with the answer to your question. Except that logic problems didn't lie. And one of these people, these nice, ordinary people, did. One of them lied, and murdered, and sat back growing fat and rich while he was locked up for years and years. You deserved to die if you did that to someone.

Jan was walking up the road to meet the car as he drove back down. He stopped, and slid over to the passenger seat.

'Keys,' she said, handing him the house keys. 'And watch.'

He wondered if he should buy her one. It could be that she just didn't wear one because she hadn't got one. He didn't think she'd be the gold bracelet type, she's probably like a big one. One of those big digital ones that he saw in the jeweller's. But maybe she didn't like wearing one. He'd have to ask.

He glanced at the time as he put the watch on his own wrist. 'Lunch,' he said. 'The Old Mill restaurant's just along the road, if it still exists.'

'It does,' Jan said. 'Aren't you going to ask for the result of your experiment?'

He didn't really have to ask. If it had failed, she would still be looking out of the window.

'I saw you after about six minutes,' she said. 'Just for a moment. Then you went out of sight.'

He nodded. 'I thought so,' he said.

At the restaurant, they were given a table outside, over the huge wheel which turned lazily and to no useful effect in the slow-moving river.

The creaking of the mill wheel and the sound of the water should have soothed him. Having lunch with Jan in the middle of the countryside he had missed so much should have pleased him. Even the sun broke through the clouds for him, but it didn't help. Because now they had all told their stories. And his final test had proved everything, and nothing.

'Shall we walk it off by the river?' Jan asked.

'Good idea,' he said, automatically falling in with her wishes. He had no wishes left.

So they walked along the river bank, through grass that grew soft and green and long. Birds sang, the river sang. Jan carried her sandals and walked barefoot.

He wasn't going to give up. One of them had done it. One of them had sent him to prison. One of them was laughing at him. They were telling him things; damn it, they were telling him more than he could cope with. And none of it would have made any difference.

She sat down, and smiled up at him. He sat beside her, pulling a blade of grass out, moodily flicking it backwards and forwards.

'Did it prove anything?' she asked at last.

'What?' he said.

'The business at the house,' she said, as patient as he was perverse.

'It proved that they're all telling the truth,' he said, lying back in supposed relaxation, the blade of grass in his mouth, his hands behind his head.

'All?' she asked, looking at the river.

'As far as I can make out,' he said.

'Bill . . . ' she turned to him.

'Yes?' he said, when she didn't go any further.

'Oh, nothing.'

He looked up at her. Nothing. It had all come to nothing, and he couldn't let that happen. Somewhere, someone had told lies. It must be there. It had to be there. And Allsopp, where did he come in? Blackmail? It must have been. Somehow, he knew who the real killer was. That was why he was dead. And he wasn't giving up. He was going to smoke out his quarry, this monster, and put it to death. And enjoy it.

His eyes were still on her. She smiled, and bent over him, taking the blade of grass from his mouth, and he pushed her away angrily. 'Don't do that,' he said, getting to his feet.

'Why not?' she said, scrambling up, and running after him as he strode away towards the car. She caught his arm, making him turn. 'Why not?' she asked. 'You want me. I know you do.'

'I don't want you! Can't you get that into your head? I don't want you!'

She dropped her hand, and he walked quickly away. In the car, he lit a cigarette and waited for her. He didn't want her. She came to him in dreams, and that was enough.

She got into the car, and pulled on her seat-belt. 'Bill,' she said. 'You can't stay this uptight.'

He mashed out the cigarette in the ashtray.

'You have to relax,' she said. 'Let yourself go.'

'With you?'

'With anyone. Do something, anything. Go to the pictures, read a book, I don't care. Play pool, go fishing. Do what other people do. Just do something to forget all this for a couple of hours.'

Holt shook his head. 'I haven't had a waking moment when I haven't thought about all this, as you call it.' He looked at her. 'Not since the instant she made that phone call,' he said.

'I know,' she replied. 'And it's wrong, Bill.'

124

'Prison's screwed me up. You told me.'

'Hasn't it?'

'Because I don't want to leap on you?'

'No,' she sighed. 'Because you don't want to do anything but read these bloody papers and talk to a whole lot of people who wish you were dead. Because you have to take some time off from it.'

'No,' he said. 'No. One of these people is lying.'

'I know,' she said. 'And we will find out the truth. But it's eating you up. Look,' she said. 'It's summer, it's warm and sunny, and you're out.' She sat back. 'And you won't enjoy it.'

'That's what Spencer said,' he muttered, as she drove off. 'I'm not out.'

She stopped at a place that did a 24-hour developing service. Holt wondered why people wanted one. 'They might not come out,' he said, handing her the film.

'Of course they will,' she said.

She drove back to the hotel, talking about her parents, trying to place the old man. Holt wasn't listening. He knew what she was trying to do. That was why she had borrowed the camera, to try to take his mind off his hunt. She was trying to take his mind away from where it had to be.

'It has to be Bryant,' he said, as she pulled into the car park of the George.

'He didn't have *time*,' she said.

'He had time to get there and back if he drove fast.'

'You can't *do* what happened to Alison in no time at all!' she shouted, then closed her eyes. 'I'm sorry,' she said. 'But it's true.' And her face was serious and sad, as it had been before.

'One of them is lying,' he said obstinately.

'There is someone else, Bill,' she answered.

'Don't say it, Jan,' he warned her.

'But I have to say it! You told me yourself that she used to go —'

'Not a word!' he shouted.

'But she was in Leicester; she must have had to pass the house on her way back.'

'Stop it, Jan.'

'You look at that letter from Allsopp. Look at how it's addressed!'

'Not another word!' he roared, his face close to hers. 'Do you understand?'

Jan closed her eyes, and he got out of the car.

She opened her door as he passed. 'Listen, Bill, tomorrow I've —' she began, but he slammed the car door shut, and walked away, into the hotel.

From the far end of the lobby he could hear the bar chat, as a Hooray Henry asked for the same again. It was cool and dark in the old hotel, and he stood for a moment with his hand on the polished wood of the bannister, feeling its round smoothness. It soothed him a little, like one of Cartwright's executive toys. No, he decided. He didn't need a drink. He went upstairs, and locked his door firmly.

Locking Jan out? Locking out what she had said? It was nonsense; it made even less sense than any of their other theories. Wendy! Wendy was the only one who had believed him, the only one who had come to see him. He had never considered her, not for a moment, and he wasn't going to start now, just because Jan thought he should.

What was she saying? That *Wendy* had deliberately set a trap for him, and watched him jailed? It was a monstrous suggestion. A monstrous, wicked suggestion. He closed his eyes, his mind assaulted by images.

Alison, not looking at him, saying she was sorry. Allsopp's empty caravan, the blood, the policemen at the door. Polite, and immovable. Bryant giving evidence, looking pale and ill; Cartwright and Cassie, listening gravely. Wendy, looking over at him, always there. Always encouraging him. Always believing him.

He'd understood Bryant's bitterness, accepted Cartwright's hostility and Cassie's venom. He'd been grateful for Spencer's indifference. One of them was a fraud; he'd known that all along. But he'd never given a thought to it being Wendy, and he wasn't going to now.

More images, more memories. Prison, stretching out in front of him. The agonising fear, the desperate protest on the roof. Jan

126

flitted into his mind, and he banished her. Locks, bars, old buildings, new buildings. Good screws, bad screws; he'd never thought he'd call them that, but he did. In the end, you conform. Jan, coming every day, just to be there. She said he had to consider Wendy, and he wouldn't.

Other prisoners, some hard cases, some frightened and lonely. Prison governors, prison visitors, his solicitor, Wendy. Wendy, giving him all the gossip, keeping him in touch. Wendy.

The moment when he knew his application was successful. No celebrations, no new hope. Just a longing for the date to come around, so that he could put his plan into operation.

And Jan, turning up from nowhere. Giving him hope. But she had no right to suggest such a thing.

Cassie, Bryant, Cartwright, Spencer, Wendy. He had listened, and watched, and he had believed them. But he hadn't really spoken to Wendy. He had just listened to a woman he hadn't recognised; a woman who sounded a little ruthless.

No! It couldn't have been Wendy . . . it couldn't. It mustn't be Wendy. How could he deal with Wendy?

Was that it? Was that why Jan had made him so angry? Because he couldn't deal with it? He lifted his head, and looked at himself in the mirror. He could deal with it. If she did that to him, then what couldn't he do to her? The others had told him things. She hadn't. She'd told him about *now*, but nothing about then. And if he had to do it, he would. Because he couldn't live with the pain. The knot was strangling him, and there was only one way to untie it. He could deal with Wendy.

He must have all the information now. He could begin ticking off the boxes. One of them was lying, but no matter. That was just another piece of information. Collate, evaluate, and compare. See which version jars with all the others. Sort out the truth from the lies.

Three weeks. He'd learned more in three weeks than he had in the thirty years before he went to prison. More than he needed to know, more than he wanted to know. But some of it was relevant, something *did* make a difference. His eyes focussed again on his own image in the mirror.

Collate, evaluate, compare. And kill.

Thirteen

It was mid-afternoon when he heard her knock. He was stretched out on the bed, reading the morning paper, but not assimilating the words. It was just something to do until it was time to go. She knocked again, and he swung his legs off the bed. He got to the door and unlocked it as she was trying the handle; it swung open. The silk blouse and brown skirt. She didn't come in.

'I've come to say I'm sorry,' she said.

He walked back into the room, leaving the door open. 'What for?' he asked.

'What I said last night.' She came in then, closing the door quietly, carefully.

'No need to apologise,' he said stiffly. 'You're right. Trust no one.'

She sat, not on the bed, but on the chair. 'I shouldn't have said it,' she said. 'And I'm sorry.'

'Don't be.' He walked over to the window and looked out at yet another hot, heavy day. 'Why the interview clothes?' he asked.

'I've been for an interview,' she said.

He frowned.

'At the *Courier*. I might be getting my old job back.'

No air. There was no air in this bloody room.

'I tried to tell you yesterday,' she said.

He pushed the old sash window up as far as it would go.

'He said it would be a while before I know if I've got it.'

He pulled at his tie. It was choking him.

'He said I'd been there so often lately I might as well work there.'

Then she ran out of things to say about the interview. 'Is there anything I can do?' she asked.

'Like what?' He didn't look round.

'Anything,' she said.

'You can pick up those photographs, I suppose.' He heard her come across the room towards him, and glanced at her. She shouldn't be here. 'Collate, evaluate, compare,' he said. 'I've done that.'

'And?'

'And I've proved nothing. So there's nothing for you to do.'

'Can I stay?'

'What's the point?' He leant on the window, and looked across the cobbles to where the Friday market was in full swing. He could just hear the cries of the stall holders above the rattle of an idling diesel engine.

She moved closer, looking out of the window with him. 'I don't think you should be alone,' she said.

'Why?' he asked. 'What am I to you, anyway? Why did you come here?'

She moved away from him, and sat on the bed. 'Because I heard you were out,' she said quietly, almost to herself. 'Because I'd never forgotten seeing you on that roof.'

No one had listened. He turned his back on the window and leant back on the sill.

'Because I wanted to know what you were like,' she said. 'I didn't know I'd feel like this.' She looked up. 'I'm sorry.'

He drummed his fingers on the window sill, as he fought the pain. No one had listened. He'd listened to them – he'd listened to their stories, but no one had listened to his. No one listened to anyone any more. Not to anyone.

Not to politicians, he thought, pushing himself away from the window. Not to teachers, or doctors. Not judges. Not policemen or vicars or peace protesters. No one. They listened to people with guns and bombs. They spent days talking to them while their poor bloody hostages fried on desert runways.

So if they were frightened of him, so much the better. They'd listen to him. He paced from the window to the door, and back again. But he didn't want them to listen, not any more. He didn't need guns and bombs to make them listen. He'd got a bomb, ticking away inside. And they'd hear it, when it exploded, whether they were listening or not. Window, door, window.

'Bill, you should try to relax.'

129

He stopped pacing. 'How?' he asked. 'By going to bed with you?'

'It might help,' she said.

'No thanks.'

She stood up. 'I'll go and get the photographs then,' she said philosophically, and went towards the door. She turned back. 'I don't have any money,' she said.

He pulled out his wallet, and handed her a ten-pound note. He didn't lock the door after her this time.

He lit a cigarette, his hand trembling slightly. Hot, sweaty, trembling; that wasn't the way. He had to look in control, be in control, stay in control, until he did it. He had thought about a gun. He even knew where he could get one – here, now. He could still get it. But he wouldn't. Guns could be traced. Guns were dangerous. He wouldn't need a gun. He was harder and stronger than any of them. She shouldn't be here, he thought, dragging on the cigarette. She shouldn't be with him. There must be someone she should be with. He crushed out the cigarette, and went back to the window.

No one had listened to him. They had listened to the prosecution.

' . . . and in the first statement given to the police by Holt, no mention was made of sexual intercourse having taken place, or of the subsequent telephone call. Indeed, in the first statement, he made no mention of having been to Mrs Bryant's house at all. Only when forced to by the sheer weight of evidence against him, did Holt admit to what had gone on between him and Mrs Bryant. Now, it may seem to you that Mrs Bryant's action immediately after their encounter – if *I* may use a euphemism . . . '

This was a joke at the expense of Holt's counsel, who had grave difficulty in calling a spade a garden implement.

' . . . was provocation, and indeed, if she had been killed there and then in a single moment of rage, it may have been thus regarded. But she was not killed there and then. She had got up, put on her bath-robe, and gone downstairs. The degree of force

130

necessary to render her unconscious would have satisfied any sudden and uncontrollable violent rage. But she was strangled. Mrs Bryant was killed, not in a moment of rage, but in cold blood.'

And it went on, and got worse.

' . . . Michael Allsopp was killed in almost exactly the same way as Mrs Bryant. There is no evidence of a struggle. One blow, this time with an iron bar, occurred within the caravan, and would almost certainly have knocked Allsopp unconscious. He was then taken out of the caravan, and strangled. Again, this is evidence of premeditation, of a ruthless and determined killer. Holt's car was seen outside the caravan, his fingerprints were found inside. The sleeve of his jacket bore traces of blood which matched Allsopp's blood.

'I suggest that spurred on by his quite unfounded feelings of guilt, Michael Allsopp did indeed carry out some further investigations into Mrs Bryant. And that when he wished to put some questions to the defendant, Holt panicked. He assumed, mistakenly, that Allsopp had been watching Mrs Bryant that day, and he went to the caravan with the express intention of killing Michael Allsopp.

'Both of these killings were done by a cold-blooded murderer, and I urge you to find the defendant guilty on both counts.'

Holt sat and listened, his hands over his face in the way that he'd been advised against. It looked like the action of a guilty man, he'd been told.

She was crossing the cobbles, looking up. She waved, but he didn't wave back.

He was still at the window when she came in, and handed him the photo wallet. 'Have you looked at them?' he asked.

'No. Here's your change.'

'Keep it. You must have some out-of-pocket expenses.'

She turned away sharply, and put the money on the dressing table.

Holt looked through the snaps. 'Here you are,' he said, handing her one of the old man. 'That one's quite good.' He found the one of her, and held it in his hand. And one of a lot of grass and grey sky. He picked up his jacket, and put the two photographs in his pocket, with the one of Alison.

'Are you going somewhere?' she asked.

'I'm going to see Bryant,' he said. 'At half past four. I've made an appointment.'

'What are you going to do?' she asked, her eyes worried, her voice full of suspicion.

'You can come, if you like,' he said. 'Find out.'

So she came with him, to Greystone, to Bryant's office.

Bryant stood up when he saw Jan. 'At least you've persuaded him to make appointments,' he said.

Jan stood by his side, watching him, not really listening to Bryant.

'What do you want now?' Bryant said, turning to him, dropping the welcoming manner.

Holt held up his hands in surrender. 'Nothing,' he said. 'Nothing more. I just thought that you ought to be the one to know that I'm leaving.'

Jan frowned slightly.

'Leaving?' Bryant said, and he couldn't keep the relief out of his voice, though for some reason he did try.

'You're all so polite,' Holt said. 'So courteous. So co-operative. I understand it's because you regard me as an escaped lunatic.' He leant over the desk. 'Why put up with it?' he asked. 'The man who murdered your wife coming back, making a nuisance of himself?'

Bryant picked up his glasses. 'I suppose,' he said slowly, polishing them as he spoke, 'because I hoped that you hadn't done it. That you could prove it to me.'

'And who would you rather had done it?' Holt asked.

'No one, of course.' Bryant folded his glasses. 'I hoped – I suppose – that Wendy was right. That someone had just –'

'Had just killed Alison and Allsopp and moved on,' Holt finished. 'But it wasn't like that, was it?'

'Are you admitting that it was you?' Bryant asked.

Jan hadn't moved. Didn't even seem to be blinking.

'No,' said Holt. 'I didn't do it. I'm telling you that I couldn't

132

find out who did. I'm telling you that either you're a murderer, or you're working with one.'

He walked to the door, with Jan following him.

'So I'm leaving,' he said. 'You can pass on the good news.' He opened the door.

Bryant stood up. 'Jan,' he said. 'I . . . I honestly believe you'd be safer staying here.'

She looked at him coldly. 'Do you?' she said, and went out.

Holt smiled briefly. 'She doesn't agree,' he said.

'I hope she's made a wise decision,' Bryant said. 'I know you have.'

Jan was waiting beside the car when he came down the stairs into the murky car park. She didn't speak as he approached; he got into the hot, airless car, and leant over to unlock her door. She ran down the window as soon as she sat down, and Holt followed suit.

Greystone's business, so important to Bryant, still went on above their heads. It was a terrible waste of resources, Holt thought idly. All those machines just sitting there eight hours a day. You would think they could be put to good use. You would think that Spencer, entrepreneur extraordinary, would have thought of some money-making scheme for unemployed vehicles.

'What are you going to do?' Jan asked again, breaking into his short holiday from death.

'What I said.' He swung the car out into the light. 'I'm leaving.'

Out, past the cows.

'When?' she asked.

Cows were happy as long as there was grass to eat.

'As fast as I can pack.'

Cows didn't have bombs ticking away inside them.

'What about me?' she asked.

Cows didn't have knots being pulled so tight that they wanted to scream.

'What about you?'

Cows didn't scream.

'Are you leaving me?'

'Yes,' he said, putting his foot down as they got on to the new, fast road into the centre of town.

133

Jan went quiet. No more questions.

As they came up to the petrol station, he glanced at the gauge. He'd better fill the tank. He wasn't sure how far he'd be driving.

He had to wait for a pump; people milled round, people who didn't have to think about murder all the time. People with families, people with dogs. A woman driving an open pick-up with a sofa on it. If the rain came, it would get ruined. A man was at the air-pump, wrestling with it, trying to unsnarl the non-snarl cable. Holt glanced at Jan, but she looked out of the side window, away from him.

A lorry hissed to a stop by the diesel, and the driver got out. He was about thirty, thought Holt. How would he feel if someone picked him up now and threw him in prison until he was forty-five? Wouldn't he want to kill? And he could, thought Holt, watching him. Big hands, strong arms. He looked at his own hands on the steering wheel. They could choke someone's life away.

For the first time, for the first time ever, he thought about Alison as victim. In his bewildered mind, she had always been the one who caused it all, the perpetrator. Now, he thought of how frightened she must have been, being attacked, being hurt, being killed by some monster. And he vowed to Alison, to beautiful, unhappy Alison, that her murderer would be frightened too. Frightened, hurt and alone. His hands gripped the wheel as he moved up to the pump. He had to make a conscious effort to take them away, and get out.

Jan slid across the seat, looking out of the open window. She didn't speak; she just watched, as he lifted the hose from the pump, and set it humming. The petrol splashed into the tank; he could smell the fumes, feel the movement. He could see Jan's eyes, dark and afraid, never letting his go. All he could think of was murder. Alison's murder, Allsopp's murder, the murder still to be done.

The rush of petrol stopped, and his eyes dropped away from Jan's. He walked quickly to the shop, waiting behind the pick-up woman. They had a fan going, but the number of people in the place made it like hell. Taking off his jacket, he wandered round, looking at the stuff on the shelves. There wasn't much to choose from.

Jan was back in the passenger seat, doing up her seat-belt.

'Hope you like chocolates,' he said. 'Thanks for your help.'

She just turned away, and looked out of the window again. He stood for a moment, the box in his hand, then shrugged, and put it on the back seat with his jacket. He pulled the car back on to the road. She didn't speak until they were in the town.

'Just drop me here,' she said, saying the words quickly, her face still turned away from him.

'Here?' he asked.

'Here.'

'But your car's at the hotel.' He drew in to the pavement as he spoke.

She opened the door. 'I'll get it later,' she said, and he could hear the tears, hear them in her voice.

The door slammed, and she walked quickly away.

Fourteen

He hadn't planned it, but it couldn't have worked out better if he had, he thought, as he opened the suitcases he had bought that morning, and carefully packed all the expensive clothes that he'd collected. He hadn't meant to make her cry; God knows, he would never have wanted to do that. But she had gone, and that was as it should be, because he needed to be alone. But he hadn't meant to make her cry.

He had to think. Just sit, and think.

Collate. He had collated.

Evaluate. They said that none of it mattered, none of it would have made any difference. None of it altered the facts. And they were right. The facts were that he had gone to bed with Alison, and she was dead half an hour later. The facts were that he had gone to Allsopp's caravan, and searched it, and he was dead already. Who Alison was seeing, what Cartwright was doing, Bryant's jealous accusations had no bearing on these facts at all. But he had a whole lot of new facts, and new facts *had* to make a difference, because he hadn't killed her.

He closed his eyes. Alison. Poor, mixed-up, sad Alison. Why did someone want her dead so badly? He opened his eyes again. Perhaps it was him. Perhaps they wanted him out of the way. But no. No. *He* had decided against calling a taxi. No one else. He had set the chain of events in motion. So what was important, and what wasn't? He had to assume that everything was important. End of evaluation.

He thought of Jan, walking away from him. Walking away in tears. She had waited in sub-zero temperatures, willing him to survive his rooftop demonstration. She had stood by him through all this, she had been there when no one else was. Trusting, never doubting, not hesitating even when Bryant was warning her not to go with him. She had done what she'd said she'd do. She had helped him, and he had hurt her. Damn it, he didn't want her, not even in his mind. Especially not in his mind.

Compare. He had compared this story with that story, this moment with that moment. And they all checked out. All their stories dovetailed. Everyone was always where he'd said he was, no matter what the source. He rubbed his eyes. They were all telling the truth. No. That was impossible. If they were all telling the truth, then the murderer was someone who just happened to be passing. Who just felt like murdering Alison. And then two weeks later, felt like murdering Allsopp. And setting him up for it. No. There was no one else involved; one of them did it.

Or all of them, he thought, and it wasn't an entirely frivolous notion. At times, it felt like a conspiracy. But it wasn't, of course. If they discussed him at all, it was to shake their heads and say that he must have lost his reason.

One of them. One of them, his family, his friends, his colleagues. One of them was a monster, for who else knew Alison and him well enough to do it, how it was done, when it was done? The thought that came in to his head then wasn't frivolous either. It was chilling.

Ralph? He had never even thought about Ralph. Of course he hadn't – he was her father, for God's sake! But who was to say that monsters didn't kill their own daughters? But Ralph wasn't a monster. He'd known Ralph all his life. He'd called him Uncle Ralph for the first fifteen years of it. He'd been a little in awe of him. He was opinionated, and easily roused to anger. But he wasn't a monster. He wasn't. He covered his mouth with his hands, feeling sick. He couldn't include Ralph. What possible reason could Ralph have had to kill Alison? He forced his mind to dig out reasons.

Money. No, don't be ridiculous.

A fight that got out of hand. What about? Cassie, of course. Hadn't Ralph tried to nip it in the bud, and failed?

Wait. Wait, he thought, clutching at a fact. It couldn't have been Ralph. Spencer had seen Ralph at Greystone, he said so. Ralph was looking for Bryant. And Ralph was there, in his office, when Spencer got there. He took his hands from his mouth, and he was breathing hard, as though he'd been running. Ralph couldn't have got to Alison and back before Spencer arrived to take his photographs. The relief made him feel weak. It wasn't Ralph, in a Victorian rage. The thought, sickening a moment ago, made him laugh, then it made him cry. This monster had to die, before he was torn in two.

He settled his account with the hotel, and carried his cases to the car. Jan's car was still there; he'd be gone by the time she came for it.

He had rung the car hire people and told them that they could pick the car up at the station the next morning. He had done it where José could hear him, because he, inveterate gossip that he was, would tell anyone who asked. He heaved the cases into the boot, and closed it. Thank God Jan hadn't come for her car.

He drove out of the car park, having to reverse and shuffle forward several times before he could actually get free of the other cars. It was still too hot, even though it was dark now. He stopped under a street light, and took off his jacket, twisting round to put it on the back seat. His eye caught the chocolates, and he threw the jacket over them. Then he reached into the pocket, and took out the photographs.

One of Alison, beautiful, laughing, happy. And one of Jan, lost, for once, for words. More beautiful. Not classic beauty, but more beautiful.

Somewhere in the mass of information, was the answer. Somewhere, hiding behind the smoke-screen, was a monster. And Holt was going to bring him to the surface.

He drove through the dark, hot, moonless night with death for company. '*I met murder on the way, it had a face like . . .*' Whose face?

His hands gripped the steering wheel and he drove fast along the dual carriageway. The orange glow appeared in the black sky, and his stomach lurched as he saw it. Closer, and the halo became defined. Closer, and the separate lights, ringing the prison, were visible. He pulled the car over on to the grass, and stared at those lights, blazing through the night, through the black, silent night. Night after night after night. Month after month, year after year.

138

A car passed him, and he watched its tail-lights as it slipped down the road to a by-passed village. Someone going home to his wife and family. Someone who could live, because he didn't have a knot being pulled tighter and tighter inside him. Someone real, someone who had never lived within those lights, locked away for something he hadn't done. Who had never lain awake, planning how to kill, how to release the knot that held in the anger and let it fly.

It had to be released. So he had to work it out. Just like he'd planned. Find the killer. All those years, all those nights of endless journeying into the past, had to be paid for. Cartwright, Spencer, Bryant, Wendy, Cassie. Something was wrong with someone's story.

And he sat in his car, watching those lights, reliving prison, comparing, evaluating, until dawn began to lighten the sky, and long tendrils of dark cloud became visible against the grey. Ticking off the boxes, until the grass showed green, and the invisible sun climbed in the sky.

But nothing altered the facts. Alison did what she did. The lights burned. Alison did what she did.

Everyone believed that he had killed Alison because of what she did. But he hadn't, of course.

He sat very still, as he thought it through. Slowly, slowly. Don't rush. Take your time, son. No hurry. One thing at a time.

He *hadn't* killed her. So what she had done to him wasn't relevant. If he had just had a cup of coffee with her, she would still be dead. Back then. Back to the station, to the moment when he had decided against calling a taxi.

If he had called a taxi, Alison wouldn't be dead. Now, all he had was a question.

The circle of lights glowed uselessly in the daylight, and were switched off. But by then, he knew the answer.

His mouth was dry, and he was stiff, as he got out of the car, and went behind a hedge. Why, he wondered. There wasn't anyone for miles, except the poor sods in Gartree. From there, he could see the car that had passed him the night before, parked on a triangle of grass beside the wall of a house. People in the country were very careless with their valuables. He could have stolen it; he intended doing something of the sort later. So he was counting on the trusting country folk, who didn't use garages.

He put his hands to his back and rubbed it as he walked back to the car. The night had been hot and sticky, and the day was worse. The weather was like him. Waiting, waiting, waiting for the right moment to let rip. And his moment was almost here. He opened the boot, and found his shaver, giving his chin a quick once-over in the driving mirror. He was just leaving town, that was all. No stubble, nothing to suggest that anything was wrong. He tucked in his shirt, and put on his jacket. Not too bad. Presentable enough for a man whose mission had failed.

But it hadn't failed. And the answer wasn't impossible. It was possible, and it was easy. Easy if you were a monster.

He turned at the sound of a car engine, and glimpsed the car leaving the village again, driving off the way it had come the night before. Late home, early start; he probably cursed his fate.

And Holt screwed his eyes up with the pain, the real physical pain, as the knot of frustrated vengeance was strained to its limit. He wanted to do it now. Go now, and let the violence out. But now he had to hold on even tighter. He had to go through with his plan. He had to do it, one step at a time, and do it right. The knot had to hold just a little longer.

It held while he drove to the station, and parked the car; it held while he sat, staring unseeingly out of the window, as the early morning train made its way to London. He was going to see his solicitor. He and the barrister had defended him to the best of their ability. They had, thought Holt. They had.

Holt's counsel got to his feet, looking less than inspired.

'The defendant in this case is, I feel, nothing more than a victim of circumstance . . . '

There was actually some smothered laughter from the gallery, and a smirk from the juror.

' . . . and of his own lack of will power.'

For a moment, Holt thought that that was all he was going to say.

'When invited by Mrs Bryant to . . . er . . . transgress with her, he readily, and ill-advisedly, acquiesced.'

140

Holt groaned silently. Half of them wouldn't understand him, even if he had anything to say.

'A moment of weakness,' he went on. 'Someone he had courted, when they were in their teens. Someone he had loved and lost. An exceptionally beautiful woman. That does not excuse what he did, but it explains it. The prosecution have leant on the fact that Mr Bryant believed as early as March of last year that his wife was having an affair. They have suggested that my client was in the habit of . . . er . . . seeing Mrs Bryant. That they had had some sort of row which had ended in her "paying him out", so to speak.

'But they have signally failed to prove this to be the case, and indeed, it was *not* the case. This was the only time that Mr Holt and Mrs Bryant, at any time in their long association, had . . .'

Everyone was waiting for the next euphemism.

' . . . had sexual intercourse,' he said.

There was real laughter, and the clerk had to quieten them down. Holt buried his face deeper in his hands.

'My client was already startled, and flattered, by her offer. He took her up on it, and when she did what she did he was indeed shocked. Stunned. There seemed no reason for it. His only thought was to get away.

'So of course his fingerprints were in the house. Of course there were fibres from his clothes on her clothes. But there were no such fibres on Mrs Bryant's bath-robe.'

The prosecution had already dealt with that. He'd got dressed *after* he'd strangled Alison, according to them.

'And fibres were found on the bath-robe which could not be accounted for amongst my client's clothing, all of which was examined by the police forensic laboratory. You have heard that the Bryants' house was being redecorated at the time, and that the bath-robe, hanging as it did in the bathroom, which was being renovated, could have been handled by a workman, or indeed a visitor to the house. But a bath-robe is surely a very personal piece of apparel, and not likely to be handled by all and sundry?'

Holt's hands slid down his face, pulling down the skin under his eyes, as he looked at the jury.

'And the other fingerprints found in the house,' he went on,

141

'have not all been identified.'

They wouldn't, the prosecution had said. Not with all the comings and goings of the workmen, some of whom had moved on.

'So there is conflicting evidence.' He cleared his throat. 'And I ask you to look upon the likelihood of the prosecution's case. Mrs Bryant was found wearing the bath-robe mentioned. My client states that when he left, she was still in bed . . . um . . . unclothed. Now, if Mrs Bryant had intended dressing, would she not have done so? If she had intended taking a bath, would she not have remained upstairs, where the bathroom is? She was clad in only the bath-robe; she wore no slippers or shoes on her feet. Would she have chosen to go downstairs thus attired?

'I suggest that she did not. I suggest that Mr Holt left her as he says he did, and that she did one of two things. One: she heard someone at the door, and put on the bath-robe in order to answer it. The prosecution have attempted to refute this, by bringing a forensic expert to tell us that only Mr Holt's fingerprints were found on the knob of the Yale lock on the door. But as we have also heard, Mrs Bryant did not keep her doors locked when she was at home. Therefore, she would have no need to touch the Yale lock, and would have opened the door just by its handle. And there were a number of fingerprints on the handle, most of which were not clear enough for identification.'

He seemed to think he'd scored a point. Holt didn't. The jury didn't.

'Two,' he continued. 'Since she was in the habit of leaving her door unlocked, she may have heard an intruder, and put on the bath-robe to investigate.'

Muffled laughter again.

'Silence in court!'

The lawyer's shoulders were beginning to sag, as he got to the impossible part. 'Obviously, my client spoke to no one about his . . . dalliance with Mrs Bryant.'

He'd get through the whole thesaurus at this rate, Holt thought sourly.

'He invented a story for his wife to cover the absence of the wedding present. He lied about what he'd done, and where he

142

had been. And when he discovered what had happened to Mrs Bryant, he foolishly persisted in that lie. Understandably, however. Mr Holt did not know what had happened to Mrs Bryant, only that he had not been involved. He thought – understandably again – that her husband may have been; a belief to which the police inclined at the outset of their enquiry. And he thought that his best course of action was to say nothing. Silence isn't always golden, but it seemed so to him.'

Holt tensed up.

'He then received the letter from Mr Allsopp. If, as has been suggested, he believed Mr Allsopp to be a threat, would he not have engineered circumstances of his own choosing for this meeting, rather than call on Mr Allsopp at the time and place of Mr Allsopp's choice? Of course he would. But he merely did as Mr Allsopp had requested, hoping that there he could find some avenue of escape from his terrible dilemma. His were the actions of a man guilty only of an indiscretion, seeking the proof that he needed to exculpate himself from any complicity in this most abhorrent crime . . .'

And so he went on, his voice becoming less and less confident, the words becoming more and more obscure. And Holt knew then that he'd had it.

The train was faster, these days, and it was still early when he arrived at his solicitor's house, breaking into his Saturday morning activities with his family. Other people had families. Holt informed him that he had been unable to make a go of it at home, and was going to stay in London for the time being. His solicitor was pleased – he was sure it was the right decision. He would make all the arrangements with the probation people. He wouldn't have to see anyone until next week anyway. He told his solicitor that he would be staying at an hotel, and gave him the address.

He checked into the hotel, and took a room for an indefinite period. He unpacked his suitcases, putting things neatly on hangers and in drawers. And he put a change of clothing into a weekend bag that he'd bought in Woolworth's.

Then out, to see an old acquaintance, running him to earth

through the landlord of the pub that he'd been told to call at if he ever needed help. The old acquaintance, for a generous inducement, guaranteed to provide him with a lady of doubtful virtue but no criminal record who would vouch for his prolonged presence in her company if asked. Holt could trust them; he knew that now. They were good, honest villains who had a price, and if you paid it, their services were yours. People masquerading as monsters. Not the other way around.

And he bought something for Jan. He would send it to her, when it was all over.

He caught the last train back, but he got off at the stop before.

In the darkness, he walked. It was eight miles to where Allsopp had lived. Eight miles to the old station, which would afford him shelter, and a hiding place. He walked along the embankment, slowly, conserving his energy. He had hours to go, and he could spend as long as he liked getting there. He didn't meet anyone on the way. He stopped often, to rest his feet, and to think of what he was to do. To savour what he was to do.

He perspired as he walked. His feet made no sound on the grassy embankment, and he moved up and out of sight when a night train came roaring past. The moon rose, visible tonight as the clouds thinned, and the night air freshened. The weather had changed its mind, but he hadn't. The plan was working. The plan, which had had its beginnings in the nightmare of solitary confinement, was coming to its climax. He just had to wait. Until four o'clock, when it would be almost dawn. Still dark enough to steal a car unnoticed, to drive away with no one hearing. Dawn when he did it, when he untied the knot, and let the fury go. Dawn. Light enough, morning enough, to put on a jogging suit, and join the Sunday morning fitness freaks.

And all the time, he was in the arms of a lady of the night in London.

A monster in its lair, imagining itself safe. A monster who would be startled, then hurt, then frightened, then dead. Like Alison. Just like Alison.

He'd taken lessons from minders, from house-breakers, from car thieves. That last had been at the open prison; he had even practised on a visitor's car. He didn't steal it, of course. But he could have. And he'd learned how to kill from the monster itself.

The judge had remarked on the finer details, particularly of Alison's murder. No special weapons to be got rid of, and possibly found, and traced. No blood to splash and give the game away. No struggle, to leave marks. Simply surprise your victim with the suddenness and ferocity of attack, and render unconscious. Then, with no resistance other than the body's own automatic survival responses, choke the life away.

It was three o'clock when he arrived at the station, bathed in moonlight, abandoned and still. He wanted to go now, *now*, and do it, and let the pain out. But he mustn't. One hour. Just one hour.

As he walked along the platform in the moonlight, his heart began to pump faster, and he clenched and unclenched his fists as the knot grew impossibly tight and hard. Inside. He must get inside, into the waiting room, out of sight. He pushed the door, scraping it along the concrete. The pale rays from the moon lightened the shadows.

And one of them moved.

Fifteen

'Hello, Bill.' Jan stepped out to where he could just see her in a thread of moonlight.

His heart hammered, his legs felt like jelly, and he put his hands on either side of the door for support. 'How in God's name?' he gasped, but his breath failed him. He stopped, shaking his head, taking time to get his breath back, to stop his thoughts racing. 'How the hell did you find me?' he shouted, his words echoing round the deserted station. But there was no one to hear.

'The same way I found you in the first place,' she said steadily. 'I followed you.'

No. No, that wasn't true. He looked over his shoulder, out at the tracks, gleaming in the moonlight, as though he might see her magic train. But there was nothing. Just the empty platform on the other side, the fence, and the bushes that hid the station from the road. He looked back at her. 'How?' he said, taking one hand from the door as his legs stopped quivering. '*How?*'

'I spent the night with you at Gartree,' she said, and her voice was clear and quiet, coming out of the darkness. He couldn't see her face, not properly. Just her outline, ghost-like and unreal.

He shook his head. 'I'd have seen you,' he said.

'You did.'

His other hand still gripped the door frame. The car? The car he'd seen? His heart still pumped, pumping the blood back into his brain. 'That wasn't your car,' he said.

'I hired a car,' she said. 'I can be very devious.'

It still didn't make sense. That car hadn't followed him. He'd have seen; he had been watching out. He had had to be careful; someone might have put the police on to him. He had been *watching*. 'I'd have seen you,' he said, his voice thick. 'You weren't behind me.'

146

'Not once you were on the Leicester road, I wasn't,' she said. 'I knew where you were going.'

He let go of the door, and walked in, beyond the scope of the moonlight. He could see her, but she couldn't see him; his clothes were dark. A killer's clothes.

'José told me what you'd arranged about the car,' she said.

His clever stroke. Make sure José knew, that everyone knew he was leaving.

'So I got to the station before you did.'

London? How could she have followed him in London? It was hard enough to get one cab, never mind another one for following purposes. Even Jan, even resourceful, clever, quick-thinking Jan couldn't do that. He wished he could see her properly. 'London,' he said. 'You couldn't have followed me.'

'I didn't try.'

The pain, knocked away by the jolt of seeing her, was back. Tearing at him.

'I knew you'd be back,' she said. 'You hadn't given up. You're too obsessed to give up. So I just waited at St Pancras. Near the platform.'

He didn't speak.

'Someone tried to sell me some pot,' she said, conversationally. 'I got propositioned. I got one or two funny looks, and a concerned — '

'All *right*!' he roared, and the word echoed.

'But I waited,' she said. 'And you did come back.'

She shouldn't be here.

'When I saw you get off the train, I knew you must be coming here. So I stayed on, and drove back.'

She could ruin everything. All his planning. 'You think you're so clever,' he said, his voice low. 'Second guessing me.' His voice grew louder. 'It wasn't clever. It was stupid. It was bloody stupid!' he shouted.

'Do you think so?' she said, and her voice was hard. Not angry, not hurt, as it was when she walked away from him. Hard, and uncompromising and steady. He stood for a moment, thinking furiously, his breathing painful and heavy. The moonlight had

147

shifted, and he could see her more clearly. 'Go,' he said. 'Just go. Go.'

She didn't move, she didn't speak.

'*Go*!' he shouted, and the word hurt as it came out. 'Just leave,' he whispered. 'Go.'

His shoes kicked up grit as he began to pace, saying the word with each footfall, like a drum-beat. 'Go,' he said. 'Go. Go.'

'Do you think I don't know?'

Her voice, raised against his, stopped him in his tracks. He spun round. 'You don't know. You don't, you don't know!'

'I saw the way you looked,' she said. 'And it frightened me. I know what you're going to do, and I'm not going to let you do it.'

He stared at her, smiling. 'You can't stop me,' he said, incredulously, almost laughing. No one could stop him. He couldn't be stopped, and he couldn't wait. He couldn't wait. It didn't matter. It would still work. He had to go. Now. *He* had to go. Not her, not her.

'You can't leave, not now,' he said. 'You'll have to stay here. But I'm leaving.'

'I won't let you go, Bill.' Her voice rose. 'You're going to kill someone, and I won't let you do it.'

'No,' he said. 'Not someone. Some*thing*. A monster.'

She moved towards him. 'They'll send you back to prison,' she said.

'No! No. I won't get caught. I know how it's done. I've been taught by experts.'

'Your experts were all in jail.'

'Except one!' he roared. The one who had called on poor, unsuspecting Alison, and snuffed her out like a candle. The one who had crashed an iron bar down on Allsopp's head. The one who slept soundly, no doubt, right now. Who would be surprised to see him. Who would be begging, before Holt had finished. Frightened, and hurt and alone. Like Alison.

'I'm owed a murder,' he said. 'I'm *owed* a murder!'

'No,' she said. 'They'll send you back to prison.'

But he wouldn't get caught. She didn't understand. He had to go, now. He had to find a car. He turned away, towards the door. He'd meant to check out cars, see which one to take, but she'd upset his planning. He'd have to go now. It might take a while to find one.

But he didn't have to steal a car now. He wheeled back to face her. 'Give me your car keys,' he said.

'What?'

'Keys, keys!' he said, holding out his hand. 'Give me your car keys!'

'No,' she said, backing away into the shadow.

He reached out and caught her arm. 'Give me the keys,' he said, pulling her back as she tried to twist away from him. He pushed her against the wall, searching with his free hand in her pockets. His hand closed round the plastic tab, and he drew the keys out, and released her. 'You stay here,' he said, ramming them into the coin pocket of his jeans. 'Do you understand? Don't move from here. Not until it's daylight.'

He went to the door, but she was there before him, slamming it shut, plunging them in darkness.

'Get away from the door.'

It was time.

'You're not going,' she said.

'Get away from the door!' He grabbed her, dragging her towards him. He could feel her body against his, her breath on his face. The door opened a crack and stuck. She was getting in his way. She shouldn't be here, close, so close, in the darkness. She mustn't stop him now. She shouldn't be here, getting in his way. Trying to stop him. He couldn't be stopped.

'I'll tell the police,' she shouted, and his hand stopped its frantic tugging at the jammed door.

'I mean it,' she said quietly, into the sudden stillness.

In that frozen moment, all he could feel was the pain, throbbing like a heartbeat, burning through his mind, as he dragged her to the ground, pulling at her clothes. Burning through his body, as she struggled to get away from him, fighting him, trying to make him stop. But he didn't stop, and it could have been anyone, anyone at all, as he thrust himself into her until the rage was gone, and he lay on the floor, breathing hard, his mind empty. He wanted it to stay that way for ever.

He could hear her, as she slowly got to her feet. He could hear her as she walked away. He could hear her pulling at the door until it finally gave, dragging across the floor. Then he was in darkness, hearing only his own breathing.

For a long time, he lay there in the darkness. Perhaps he fell asleep. Perhaps he was asleep. He was, he was asleep. It was just another dream. It *was*. It hadn't happened; he hadn't done that. He was alone, in the dark. He hadn't done that. He sat up, awake in the darkness. It was just another dream.

But the darkness wasn't real; it was his darkness, his eyes screwed up to block out the memory, his hand over his face. When he took his hands away, he could see the pale sky through the half open door, as the sun rose. That was real. That was *real*. It had happened.

He remained where he was, waiting in the shadow, until the sun began to creep through the door, to glimmer through the wooden slats on the windows. And still he waited, watching the patch of sunlight slowly move over the floor, until it lit the scuff marks in the grit. Then he looked away, and stood up, pushing his shirt into his jeans, zipping them up.

The sun's rays landed on the pile of rubbish, the bench. They travelled over the obscenities scrawled on the wall, and he began to shake. His plan. His plan belonged on that wall, belonged with those marks on the floor. He had dragged Jan into his sunless prison. Jan, whose love had been offered to him without question.

He pushed through the door, into sunlight that hurt his eyes, and he didn't see her at first. But she was there, on the bench, staring towards the railway lines, and he wanted to die, as he walked towards her. To die before he got there. But he didn't.

She was aware of his presence, but she didn't look at him, didn't speak. He couldn't look at her. 'I thought you'd gone,' was all that came out of his mouth.

'I didn't have the sodding keys.' She barely whispered the words, but anger shook in her voice.

'Oh. Christ. No . . . I . . . ' He dug in the coin pocket, and took them out. 'I . . . ' he began again. 'Oh God,' he said, sinking down on to the bench as his shaking legs failed him. 'I didn't do

150

that,' he said, burying his face in his hands. 'I didn't. I couldn't. I couldn't have done that.'

She didn't speak.

'It . . . it wasn't . . . ' It sounded ridiculous, but he kept going. 'It wasn't you,' he said. 'It wasn't you.'

'It felt like me.'

He drew his hands away, his fist clenched round the keys, making them dig into his palm. And he looked at her then, for the first time.

The old-fashioned shirt, dirty, with buttons missing. The white jeans, smeared with the grit and the dust from the floor. Her face was streaked with tears; her hair curled on to her collar.

'I didn't do that,' he said again. 'I couldn't have done that.'

She threw her head back and looked at the sky, as she tried to stop the tears coming again.

He screwed his eyes up, shutting out the image, shutting out the sun that lit it, clear and bright and real. He tried to find the empty darkness where he could hide. The words were inadequate and quite useless, but they were all he had.

'But I love you,' he said, and it had taken a mockery of love to make him able to say it. The man who hunted monsters couldn't say it, though he had known it; he couldn't have loved her, in case it had taken the edge off his appetite.

He opened his eyes, and held out the keys to her, but she didn't take them, didn't look at them, or him. 'Will you let me drive you?' he asked.

She got up and walked away, and he followed her to her car.

He drove slowly, carefully, still trembling, his mind in a daze. Jan sat stiff and still beside him, her hands clasped in front of her, her knuckles white with the effort of keeping control.

He was parking at the George before he realised that she didn't live there. 'Would you rather I took you — ' he began, but she just got out of the car, slamming the door. He got out and ran after her, into the hotel.

José looked up, dismayed, and came out from behind reception. 'What happened?' he asked, his arm round Jan's shoulders. 'What happened to you?'

There hadn't been a word spoken on the journey back, and there was a long moment before Jan answered. When she did, she looked at him, not at José.

'I had an accident,' she said.

'No! Are you hurt? Do you need a doctor?'

'No,' said Jan, and her hostile eyes were still on his. 'Just a hot bath.'

'Yes, yes, of course. Maria!' José called, turning towards the office, then back to Jan. 'An accident in your car?' he asked. 'Maria!' he shouted again.

Jan's gaze fell away, as she turned to José. 'No,' she said.

José's eyes flicked over to him, and back to Jan. 'What, then?' he asked. 'What happened to you?'

'I fell off a roof,' she said.

Sixteen

She had been gone, when he had come back down from his room, wearing the jogging suit that had been part of his plan. His ridiculous, murderous plan. He had stuffed his other clothes into the rubbish chute. His killer's clothes. She had had to borrow clothes from Maria.

And he had gone back up to his room and looked at himself in the mirror. A fool in a jogging suit had looked back, and he had turned away. Exhausted, he had slept, then had woken in the night. Alone in the dark. Real dark? Real. And shame had burned over him as he remembered. Remembered what he had done. Remembered the names she had called him as she had tried to fight him off. Remembered the cold, speechless anger on the long drive back to the hotel. And he had had to live with his demons until morning, only to find that sunlight made him see them all the more clearly.

He had bought some more clothes, and gone again to London, to the hotel, not sure what he intended doing. Stay there? Pack and go away somewhere else altogether?

Without conscious decision, he began to pack up his clothes again. To do what? Go back and face the monster? Go back and face Jan. He couldn't face Jan. He had to face her.

He caught the first train back, his courage ebbing away with every mile of track. Jan had given him strength. And hope. She had made herself an enemy of someone who had already murdered twice, simply by helping him.

My God. She was in *danger*. He had to warn her. He had to get her away from here. Send her away. He cursed the train as it carried on at the same speed, unaware of the urgency. He arrived at the station, and grabbed a taxi. If he had taken a taxi . . .

The driver went as fast as he could through the town, to the boarding house. Holt ran up the path, leaning on the door bell.

'What are you playing at?' Mrs Buxton was shouting, as she opened the door. 'Oh,' she said, startled. 'I thought it was kids.'

'Is Jan here?' he asked.

She looked at him warily. 'No,' she said.

'Where is she? When will she be back?'

'What my lodgers do is their business – it's none of mine, and it's certainly none of yours.'

'But it's really important that I see her,' he said.

'Are you this man she goes about with?'

'I expect so,' he said.

'Then I don't think she wants to see you,' she said coldly.

Holt felt sick. 'Look, I just have to tell her something important. I won't — '

'You're too late,' she said, interrupting. 'She's gone.'

'Gone?'

'Left,' she said triumphantly. 'This morning. I don't think she wants you bothering her again.'

'Left,' he said, feeling slightly better. She was safe, then, if she'd left. 'Would you know if she's gone back to Leeds?'

'No,' she said. 'And I wouldn't tell you if I did.'

Holt looked at the implacable face. If she said indoors by eleven, that's what she'd mean all right. 'Do you know where she is?' he pleaded, but it was no good.

The *Courier*. She had a friend at the *Courier*. She might know Jan's address. If she wouldn't see him, at least he could write to her.

But the girl at the *Courier* took away the ray of hope that Mrs Buxton had given him.

'I don't think she'll have left,' she said.

'Why not?'

She looked a little unwilling to say. 'I just don't think she's actually left here,' she said. 'If Mrs Buxton says she's left her, I suppose she has. But it seems a bit odd.'

'Why? Why don't you think she's gone?'

'Because . . .' She sighed. 'Because she borrowed some money from me, and she said she'd pay me back on Friday. She wouldn't go, not without paying me back. Certinly not without telling me.'

154

Holt sat down. 'Then where do you think she is?' he asked. 'She can't have much money left – where would she go?'

'That's what I don't understand,' the girl said. 'I'd have thought she'd come to me.'

The shops were closing as he walked back to the George. The girl had given him Jan's phone number in Leeds, but the man who answered said that she hadn't been in her flat for about three weeks.

He rang Mr Denton at the old people's home, but he didn't have an address for her parents. He put down the phone, aware that who he really needed on this job was Jan.

José was worried about him; he wasn't eating properly. Maria, more of a realist and less of a romantic than her husband, wasn't really speaking to him.

On the Tuesday, he went to everywhere in the town that took paying guests, and drew a blank each time. He even drove out to the Bryants' old house, just in case she was squatting there. He tried Leeds again, and got a woman this time. She was more chatty, and told him that she thought Jan must be on a job somewhere. Sometimes they took a few days. Or perhaps she was on holiday; she'd be sure to tell her that he rang. He tried to ask Maria if she knew where she was, but she was polite, and distant, and said that she had no idea. Did she bring your clothes back? he tried. They were old clothes. Maria had told her not to bother.

On Wednesday, he stood outside the police station for so long that he was beginning to get interested glances out of the window, but he didn't go in. What could he say? He thought someone was missing who might be in danger. And they'd ask him why he thought she was missing. The fact that she'd left the boarding house in a perfectly normal fashion wouldn't count as missing. And if he explained why she was in danger, they wouldn't listen. Or if they did, she'd only be in worse danger.

On Thursday, he tried proper hotels for miles around, and thought hard about hospitals. He went to the old people's home to talk to the old man, to see if she had any aunts or cousins that she might have gone to, but he said no. Her parents had moved here when their eldest was about four. Jan was the youngest, Holt found out. He tried to remember her as a child, but he couldn't single her out from the brood of self-confident, cheerful children that the Wentworths had produced. Mr Denton thought her family were from Lancashire originally. That's where she would have aunts and things. But he didn't know where. Why? Was she giving him the runaround? He hadn't got to worry about her. She could take care of herself at three, so she could take care of herself now.

It was dark by the time he got back to the hotel. At least he had taken his key. No need to make conversation with José, who seemed never to sleep, for fear of missing something.

Jan's hire car still sat in the car park uncollected. She hadn't been seen since Monday. He would have to go to the police. No one else was worried. Not Mrs Buxton, or Maria, or her friend at the *Courier*. But they didn't know what he knew.

Then he saw it. Jan's own car, parked beside a Rover, almost hidden from view. He didn't want to go in. But he had to. He had to face her. Where had she been? Maybe she'd brought the police. He walked slowly upstairs, and stood for a moment outside the door before going in.

She was alone. 'José let me in,' she said.

'Where the hell have you been?'

She raised her eyebrows. 'Mrs Buxton's,' she said. 'I told her to tell you I'd left.'

'I've been looking everywhere for you.'

'Were you worried about me?' she asked.

'Yes.'

'Good.'

It was no more than he deserved. His face went red as the shame claimed him again. 'You shouldn't stay here,' he said. 'It's dangerous.'

'Why? Are you going to do it again?'

He stared at her. Oh God, no. It was true. He was the only one who had hurt her. The only one who had ever been going to hurt her.

She got off the bed and came towards him. The pink vest, with

156

the denims she had been wearing the first time he saw her. She looked beautiful in them. In anything. He still had no words to say he was sorry. Desperately sorry.

'Did you want me?' he said.

'Yes.' She took his hand in hers. 'I still do.'

'No,' he said. 'You can't. Not after what I did to you.'

'It wasn't me,' she said.

'You're the one who got hurt.'

'A bit bruised,' she said. 'But I was angry. Very angry.'

Physical hurt, emotional hurt. Use the crushing mechanism . . . it was easy, easy to hurt people.

'And I wasn't even sure why,' she said. 'I knew what I was doing, going there. I knew you were half out of your mind. I thought . . . ' She looked up at him, and gave him a brief smile. 'I thought you might kill me if I tried to stop you,' she said. 'I just never thought of that.'

She still held his hand between hers, almost as though she had forgotten it was there.

'I think I felt cheated,' she said. 'Cheated out of how it should have been.'

He turned away from her.

'Maybe even cheated out of my noble gesture,' she went on. 'It all seemed so . . . so undignified.'

'Unforgivable,' he muttered.

'No.' She touched his face, turning his head so that he was looking at her. 'No,' she said again. 'Unpleasant. Shall we settle for that?'

Her other hand still held his. 'Will you do something for me?' she asked.

'Of course,' he said.

'Will you please give me a proper kiss?'

Shyly, nervously, he bent his head, and briefly pressed his lips to hers.

'Not that proper,' she said.

And this time, it was Jan. It was Jan who came into his arms, loving him, trusting him. He didn't deserve her trust, and he must have spoken the thought aloud.

157

'You didn't deserve sixteen years in prison,' she said.

He stepped back a little and looked at her. 'Maybe it was worth it,' he said.

She shook her head.

It should have been gone. The knot of pain was gone, the terrible urge to kill was gone, but the desire was still there. The cold greyness was still there, somewhere even Jan's warmth couldn't reach.

'Do you know who it was?' he asked.

'Yes,' she said.

He turned away from her, and picked up her briefcase. 'I have to prove it,' he said. 'And I can't. I can't.' Perhaps if he looked through the papers again, now that he knew what to look for, he might find a way to prove what he knew. Knew beyond a doubt. He opened the briefcase, and looked at the contents. The transcript, the newspaper cuttings. Allsopp's report, rescued from the floor by Jan, and smoothed out as best she could. Her tape recorder, her notebook, with its neat, clear entries. He felt a rush of love and remorse.

And anger. If he couldn't have revenge, he wanted justice. Real justice, with wigs and gowns and oak-panelled courtrooms. Real justice, with tradition and precedent, with rules and regulations.

Jan's hands were on his shoulders. 'Take your shirt off,' she said. 'And lie face down on the bed.' She patted him. 'Go on,' she said. 'Do it.'

He gave in, and lay down. She began to massage his back, his shoulders, his neck.

'Where did you learn that?' he asked.

'A friend.' Her fingers worked on his muscles. It hurt, but it was a good feeling.

'You'll have back trouble if you won't learn how to relax,' she said. Her fingers traced the scar on his arm. 'Did you get that in prison?' she asked.

He didn't answer. Maybe it was there to remind him of what he'd become, in prison.

'You've got to relax,' she said. 'Go to yoga or something. Learn how.'

'There's no point,' he said. 'I don't want to relax. I'm owed something. Justice. Justice, at least.'

She carried on kneading, massaging.

'And I'm not going to get justice,' he said, twisting round, catching her hand. 'Am I?'

'What about fingerprints?' she asked. 'That might prove something if they know whose to look for.'

'But they *won't* look,' he said, sitting up. 'They won't look, because I've got no new evidence. You need new evidence. Evidence that wasn't available to the jury. That's what you need for an appeal, and I don't have any evidence.'

'We'll find some,' she said and the gleam was back in her eyes.

'Don't, Jan,' he said. 'It's over. We can't prove anything.'

'My friends in Wisconsin would tell you that it's not all over till the fat lady sings,' she said.

He smiled. 'Trouble is,' he said. 'She's got one foot on the stage.'

'And we're going to leave her there,' she said.

She pushed him gently back on to the pillow, kissing him. 'Right now,' she said, 'you are going to forget all about it.'

And he did. He really did.

Seventeen

The sudden, heavy burst of rain eased off, and vanished, as all the others had done. Holt opened the window as wide as it would go. Overhead, the sky was blue, but a purple-black stain was drifting over from the east, the shafts of sunlight which broke through it only heightening its menace. The thunder had come in the middle of the night, just when no one expected it any more. It grumbled now, as Holt stood by the window, watching the Friday morning shoppers begin to fill up the precinct.

He had seen the sun rise; he had seen the stall holders arrive at the market place, shouting and laughing as they pulled wet canvas over the frames, a job so difficult that laughter was the only way to deal with it. Van doors had banged, racks of poly-thene-sheeted clothing were rattled along shiny wet cobbles. The bustling activity had awakened Jan, and they had made love again. Then, lying in his arms, it had been her turn, for once, to answer questions.

She had worked at the *Courier* for almost twelve years. In that time she had been married and divorced.

'What went wrong?' he had asked.

'He met someone else.'

She had lived with another man for almost two years. He was an osteopath, she told him, with a smile. He had taught her massage and how to cook Indian food. But they had mutually and amicably ended the relationship, just about when the *Courier* was taken over.

'Not a good period of my life,' she had said.

The new owners had brought staff with them, and offered her a job on the woman's page; the old *Courier* hadn't *had* a woman's page. She did not have a high opinion of women's pages. 'Is the rest of the paper too difficult for them?' Twelve years, and they didn't even want her to edit the damn thing, so she had said she would rather leave. She wished now that she hadn't.

There was nothing to keep her, so she went to work for the free paper in Yorkshire. The job had been brief, but she had stayed on there, doing freelance work for the dozens of new papers that were suddenly appearing.

'There must be someone waiting for you to come home,' he had said.

'No,' she'd said. 'Not now.'

He had said that her husband must have been crazy if he preferred someone else.

She had laughed. 'Haven't you noticed?' she had said. 'People don't find me that easy to live with.'

She could play the bagpipes at three o'clock in the morning and keep coal in the bath as far as he was concerned, he had told her.

'You reserve judgement,' she had said. 'You've only known me a month.' Then she'd kissed him, and claimed first crack at the bathroom.

A month, he thought, watching the threatening weather closing in again. It seemed like five minutes. It seemed like a hundred years. But it was a month. It was Friday, 25th July. On Friday, 24th July, sixteen years ago, he had phoned Greystone instead of getting a taxi. Sixteen years. Sixteen years of hell. Four weeks since he'd come back. Four weeks since he'd begun to execute his plan, and all that torture couldn't be for nothing. He had to salvage something from it all. He had to make them listen. And it was board day at Greystone again.

He opened the wardrobe door. He had to look the part. The dark blue suit, and one of the new shirts he hadn't worn yet. Pale blue? White? He chose white. Tie. He didn't have a tie that matched the suit. Perhaps the beige suit. It was lighter weight, so that might be a better idea. Then he could use the brown tie. White shirt? No. He'd wear the blue suit, and the blue shirt. But what about a tie? He could buy a tie. Dark blue with a pale blue stripe, maybe. No. He'd got the grey suit. Grey suit, blue shirt; hadn't he bought a grey woollen tie? He began looking through drawers. Yes . . . yes, he had. It was there. It would be all right.

She came out of the bathroom, and looked at the suits laid out on the bed. 'Are you having a sale?' she asked.

161

'What do you think of this tie with this suit?' he asked.

'It's fine,' she said. 'Why are you getting all dressed up?'

'I've got something to do.'

'What do you mean you've got something to do?' she asked, her voice suspicious.

'Not killing anyone,' he said, and escaped into the bathroom.

When he came out, she was sitting on the bed, and his suits were hung up on the wardrobe door.

'What are you going to do?'

Again. What was he going to do? 'Attend a board meeting,' he said. He pulled on the trousers of the blue suit, but they felt very hot and heavy, so he took them off again. The beige one would be best.

She thought about that for a moment. 'Can I come with you?' she asked.

'No.' Yes, they felt much better. Shirt . . . shirt. He took out the brown shirt.

'Why not?'

'You're not on the board.' Maybe he should wear the blue suit. 'Would this tie go with the blue suit?' he asked, holding up the grey tie.

'You're not on the board either.'

The beige suit, white shirt, brown tie. That would be all right. He ripped open the packaging of the shirt, and began removing clips and pins.

'Can I come?'

'You won't like what I'm going to do,' he said.

She laughed, but he could see her in the mirror, and she was not amused. 'I'm entitled to be in at the kill,' she said.

'So to speak?'

'So to speak.' She touched his shoulder. 'Will they still be serving breakfast?' she asked.

He pulled on the shirt, and buttoned it. It was a bit scratchy. Breakfast. He'd been up for hours, and he still had hours to wait.

He turned round. 'Probably not,' he said. 'But Maria will make you something anyway.' He smiled. 'I'm not sure whether I'll get fed,' he said. 'She's gone off me.'

'I didn't tell her,' Jan said. 'But . . . well.' She shrugged.

He saw her for an instant as she had looked at the station, and held her so close to him that she complained that she couldn't breathe.

He let her go. 'Come on,' he said, doing up his tie. 'You're hungry.'

Maria had taken to the full English breakfast as to the manner born, and Holt pushed his plate away before he had eaten a quarter of it. He watched Jan as she ate, until she told him not to, then picked up a paper and pretended to read it.

Jan poured him more tea. 'Do you want me to change into my Sunday best?' she asked.

'You're not coming,' he said.

'You'll need moral support.' She took away the newspaper. 'They might not throw you out if I'm there,' she said.

'Don't be too sure,' he said.

'Good,' she said. 'I'll go home and change.'

He waited for her to come back, and watched the rain streak the window, looking like tears. It was too bloody hot. He took off his jacket, but he could still feel his collar going limp.

He checked himself in the mirror, and pulled off the tie, unbuttoning the neck of his shirt.

That stuff didn't work, he thought, seeing the patches under his arms. He'd better change his shirt. He could wear the brown shirt. Not quite board-room style, but better.

He pulled off the white shirt. Should he put more stuff on, or have another bath? He squirted on more anti-perspirant.

The brown shirt felt cool. A tie. Damn it, he hadn't thought of that. He didn't usually wear a tie with the brown shirt.

Jan came in, without knocking, and that made him feel better.

'How did your interview go, anyway?' he asked, when he saw her.

'I'm not sure,' she said. 'I wasn't really in the mood.'

It was lunchtime, but neither of them wanted to eat again, so they waited until it was time to run through the rain to the car, time to drive through the congested, light-infested, one-way traffic out to the edge of town to where the cows were, to where

Greystone stood on its stilts. Time to put the car in its shadow, and look at one another.

'Relax,' she said, switching off the engine.

They didn't speak in the lift. Jan squeezed his hand as they walked along the corridor and into the board room.

'Good afternoon,' said Holt.

Charles, in the act of hanging his jacket over the back of the chair, looked up. 'What are you doing here?' he asked coldly.

'Bob told us you'd left,' said Wendy.

'Where is Bob?' Holt asked. 'Not late, surely?'

Bryant and Cassie came in from Bryant's office, and Cassie stopped dead when she saw him, but Bryant was by now immune to his sudden appearances.

'Can't we get some sort of court order to stop him coming here?' Cassie said.

'Now, now, cousin,' said Holt, 'that's no way to be.'

Cassie regarded him coldly. 'You've no right to be here,' she said. 'And neither has she, whoever she is.'

'Ah, yes. For those of you who don't know her, this is Jan Wentworth. She's come to see fair play, but I think she may be disappointed.'

Jan shot a look at him, but he ignored it.

'Jeff you already know,' he said, as Jeff came in, a little startled. 'Bob you know. Cassie, Charles, and my ex-wife, Wendy.'

Jan looked embarrassed.

Holt wished he could take his jacket off, but he knew there would be patches under his arms. Especially on a brown shirt. He should have kept the white shirt on. How come Charles didn't sweat? At least he hadn't put a tie on; Jan had said he was all right as he was. He crossed to the window. 'You don't mind, do you?' he said, pushing it open.

The group watched, bemused.

'Now,' he said. 'A chair for you, Jan.' He picked up one of the chairs that stood along the wall, and put it at the opposite end of the table from Bryant. 'There,' he said, as she sat down, looking at him a little nervously.

'Are you going to allow this to continue?' Cassie demanded of Bryant.

'Yes. Look, it's just not . . . ' Bryant tried, and gave up. 'Greystone business does have to go on, you know,' he said in the end.

'Of course it does, Bob. Taking care of business is first nature with you, isn't it?'

'I could have you removed.'

'You could. But I wouldn't advise it. I just want to address the board.' He put his hands in his pockets and strolled round the table as the others reluctantly took their seats.

'Sixteen years ago — virtually to the day — Alison was murdered. I'm sure none of you need reminding. Two weeks later, Michael Allsopp was murdered, and I was arrested. I was released four weeks ago. And I came here, and asked for your help. I must take this opportunity to thank you all for your co-operation.'

He stopped walking. 'If you spend day after day locked up with people, you become something of a man-watcher,' he said. 'You can tell who's going to be trouble, and who's going to be sick with fear. You can tell all sorts of things, just by watching people. Eyes,' he said, resuming his walk. 'I find eyes the best guide.'

He stopped by the bookcase, and leant an elbow on it. 'I remember Wendy's eyes used to fill with tears if she was worried about anything,' he said. 'And Bryant's, they go blank when he's lying.'

He looked at Jan. 'And Jan's go dark if she's afraid,' he said, his voice low. 'The light just goes out of them.'

He pushed himself away from the bookcase, and tapped Cartwright on the shoulder. 'Charles's eyes pop when he's angry,' he said. 'And Cassie's go bright when she's sad.'

'Fascinating,' said Charles.

'You'd be surprised what you can find fascinating when every day is the same as the next,' Holt said. 'All five thousand eight hundred and ten of them, because that's how long I was a prisoner, Charles.'

Jan's eyes dropped away from his.

165

'A reversal of the usual procedure,' he said. 'First hell. Then four weeks of purgatory. And this is day one of my life.'

'If this has got a point, do you think you could get to it?' Bryant said.

'Of course, Chairman.' Holt took a chair and sat it in the middle of the room. 'But it may take a while. You'll have to bear with me,' he said, as he straddled it. 'Back to eyes,' he said. 'Jeff's never change. But then, Jeff's a hustler. He's learned not to give himself away.'

'I'm not frightened of him, even if you are!' Cassie said. 'I'm calling security.'

'I don't think you should do that, Cassie,' said Bryant, looking fixedly at Jan as he spoke.

'So that's why you brought along a hostage,' Cassie said.

Holt looked quickly at Jan, who gave him the tiniest of winks.

'Bob thinks we'll find you with your throat cut if we don't listen to what my cousin has to say,' Cassie said to Jan. 'Doesn't that worry you?'

Jan shook her head. 'I listened,' she said.

Cassie looked back at him. 'It seems your friend has the casting vote,' she said.

'I came back to find out who killed Alison,' Holt said, and six pairs of eyes looked at him.

'It could have been anyone,' he said. 'But I never considered you, Wendy. I got very angry when it was suggested that I should.' He glanced at Jan. 'So I did consider you,' he said. 'I had to, once the suggestion had been made. And the more I considered you, the more reasonable it seemed.'

Wendy turned to face him.

'You took the afternoon off to go into Leicester,' he said. 'Shopping for something to wear to Jeff and Thelma's wedding. And you didn't get back until after I got home.'

Wendy didn't speak.

'The thing is, no one ever asked you to prove it, did they? So perhaps you weren't in Leicester that long. Perhaps as you passed the Bryants' house on your way home, you thought you'd pop in to see Alison. Show her what you'd bought. You walked in, as you always did . . . ' He stood up, and carried the chair over

166

to where Wendy sat. She turned away, and flicked the corner of a notebook with her thumb.

'Did you hide downstairs?' he asked. 'Wait until I'd gone, then jump Alison?' He sighed, and sat back. 'A little athletic, I think. But hell hath no fury and all that; perhaps that's how it was.'

The room had gone very quiet. Jan, close to him now, was watching him all the time.

'Then there was the letter,' he went on. 'It wasn't sealed. It was addressed to W. Holt; perhaps you thought it was for you. So you read it, and realised that Allsopp was dangerous. But you were at work when Allsopp was murdered, weren't you? Only, again, no one asked you to prove that. So you could have murdered him, safe in the knowledge that I'd go haring out there just after you'd taken an iron bar to him.'

Wendy clasped her hands in front of her, and didn't say a word.

'I think this is monstrous,' Charles said hotly. 'Wendy has never stopped believing in you. Is this the sort of thanks she gets?'

'That was one of the things that counted against her,' Holt said, and turned back to Wendy. 'You never believed that I might have done it, not for a minute. The evidence was beginning to convince even me, but not you.' He stood up, and pulled his chair back from the table. 'I thought that there was really only one way you could be that sure.'

He walked back up the table, as though he were pacing out a measure. 'Until I met someone who really believed in me,' he said.

Wendy's eyes slid towards Jan, who didn't see her looking, because her whole attention was on him.

'And I realised that you didn't believe in me at all. All I was ever being offered was a non-belief. You don't believe I did it, but you don't believe anyone else did either! You prefer to think that it was some wandering assassin, some sort of avenging angel. Not a real person.' He stood by Bryant. 'You don't know who did it, and you don't want to know, do you Wendy?' he said. 'When I realised that, that's when I crossed you off.'

167

Eighteen

'What sort of game are you playing?' Charles asked.

Holt ignored him, and tapped Bryant's shoulder. 'You were the ante-post favourite, if you remember,' he said. 'I overtook you in the finishing straight.'

He looked down the table to Jan, who was leaning forward, her elbows on the table, her chin on her hands.

'She rang you, after all,' he said, bending down, talking quietly. 'She told you she was in bed with another man.' He tutted. 'Not a nice thing to do. But then, what you were doing wasn't very nice, was it? Spying on her? I mean, even if she was seeing another man, couldn't you just have asked her about it? That would have been more up front, as they say in Wisconsin.'

He stood up, and flexed his back. 'But that wasn't what it was about, was it Bryant? She told you about her lovers.'

Wendy, who had been staring at her notepad, looked up quickly. Cartwright's eyes widened. Cassie closed hers.

'Now wait a minute,' said Spencer.

'She told you about Warwick,' Holt went on. 'And about me — in her own dramatic fashion — and Charles, of course,' he added carelessly, turning to Cartwright, whose neck had grown pink. 'Yes, Charles,' he said. 'Alison admitted the whole thing.'

Cassie buried her face in her hands, but no one was looking at her. All eyes were on Charles.

'She couldn't have,' Charles said.

'But she did,' Holt answered. 'Didn't she, Bob?' He turned back to Bryant.

'I won't have this,' Bryant said. 'I won't have Alison's memory —'

'Besmirched?' suggested Holt. He leant over. 'Shall I tell you something?' he said. 'So far, you're the only person I've spoken to who has besmirched her memory. Isn't that interesting?'

'I don't have to put up with this,' Bryant said.

Holt put a hand on his shoulder, and the resistance was short-lived. 'But you thought it was Cartwright she was seeing then, didn't you? So what did you do?' he asked. 'What did you do when you got that call from Alison, and Cartwright was there with you? Did you rush home, demand to know who it was this time? Knock her about until she told you? Strangle her when she did?'

Bryant snorted.

'Of course,' said Holt. 'You didn't have time to do that, did you? Charles here saw you just before seven. It just wasn't possible.'

Bryant relaxed a little.

'Unless you got someone to do it for you, of course,' said Holt. Everyone stared at him.

'Allsopp was supposed to be watching Alison the week we were in Brussels,' Holt said. 'And Charles here tells us that Alison was in his office when Warwick was run over. But that's not on Allsopp's report, is it? He doesn't mention Alison going anywhere near Greystone.'

Bryant frowned. 'I don't understand,' he said.

'No. Well, there's a theory — just a theory, of course — that you didn't employ Allsopp to watch Alison at all. You employed him to run young Warwick over. And then, you employed him to murder Alison.'

Wendy actually laughed. Bryant sat open-mouthed.

'This is Greystone, Bill,' said Spencer. 'Not the Mafia.'

Holt looked round the table. 'Any more comments?' he asked.

'I don't know why we're allowing you to do this,' Cassie said.

'But it is an interesting theory, don't you think? I mean, if Bob had booked Allsopp for a murder, and then he'd got that call, well!' He threw his hands up. 'What to do? He thought Alison was alone, and now she tells him she's got someone with her, in a manner of speaking. No wonder he disappeared sharpish, instead of establishing a water-tight alibi. He had to work out what to do.

'But there wasn't much he could do, except wait and see. And then he finds that Allsopp has actually done the job, despite complications setting in. And Allsopp tells him about me. Now then,' he said, an enthusiastic lecturer, posing hypothetical problems for his students. 'What if I had *seen* Allsopp? That would make us both dangerous. So he tricks Allsopp into writing to me, and then does away with him. Leaving me holding the iron bar, as it were. Neat?'

'Is this a serious accusation?' Wendy asked quietly.

Holt smiled. 'No,' he said. 'Just my bit of fun. Though one of you is capable of anything, so why not hiring Allsopp? Perhaps assassination was another of his hobbies — he was a great hobby-ist, that chap. Photography,' he said, counting off on his fingers. 'Blackmail . . . but I'll come to that later.' He passed Cassie as he spoke; she had gone pale. 'But he didn't kill Alison,' he said. 'Because he wasn't there.'

He tutted at the rain which swept over the fields and lashed the building. 'Very exposed here,' he said, looking out at the puddles forming in the uneven surface of the forecourt. He turned back. 'But I didn't cross you off, Bob,' he said. 'Because I couldn't think why you wanted to have a private detective watching Alison at all.'

He pulled the chair out into the middle of the room and sat down, his long legs stretched out in front of him, crossed at the ankles. 'If you wanted a divorce, there was no need to go to all that expense. Alison told you about her lovers anyway. But you didn't want a divorce, did you? You even suspected that she wasn't telling you the truth. That she was shielding someone, with all these confessions.'

He glanced over at Cassie, but she didn't react.

'And you had to know who,' he continued. 'So that you could deal with it. Scare him off, pay him off — whatever would work. Anything to hang on to your sad little marriage.'

'Is it wrong to hang on to your marriage?' Bryant asked.

'It is when you're married to a business,' Holt said. 'You didn't want competition, not until Ralph handed over the reins. Which he duly did. In April. And then you didn't give a damn what Alison was doing. You didn't even go home when you got that call.'

He stood up again, and began touring the table slowly. 'You didn't care for Alison enough to kill her,' he said. 'That's when I crossed you off.'

Bryant coughed quietly into the embarrassed silence.

170

'I think we've heard enough of this,' said Spencer.

'Do you? You were on my list, too, Jeff.'

'It's my turn, is it?'

'Yes,' said Holt. 'There were so many things I couldn't understand about you. Why did you keep quiet about seeing me with Alison? Half the police in the county were looking for the man who was with her, and you knew who it was. That puzzled me, Jeff. It really did. For sixteen years.'

'Don't get involved. That's my motto.'

'Especially when the other half of the police are looking for you?' Holt said.

This time there was real silence. No rustles, no scribbles.

'I think you'll have to clarify that,' Spencer said.

'Certainly.' Holt leant across the table, between Cassie and Charles. 'You had a meeting with Ralph and Charles. You were still driving the gas-guzzler – remember it? Yes, of course you do; we were talking about the old girl just the other day, weren't we? You had driven down from London, and stopped to have lunch, I expect. Wheeling and dealing. Too long a lunch; too much brandy. It made you late, so you were going fast, and you misjudged the turn into Greystone. The car went out of control, and you went smack into young Warwick. Is that clear enough?'

Spencer's face didn't change, but he turned his wedding ring round and round on his finger as Holt spoke.

'The police thought there were two people in the car,' Holt said. 'Because the old man heard the passenger door open. But he didn't, did he? He heard the driver's door open, of a left-hand-drive car. You thought you had no option but to get out, because someone had seen the whole thing. But then you saw his white stick, and you didn't hang around.'

Holt straightened up. 'That's how come it happened in Greystone's car park, on a Saturday. And it's how come you missed a very important meeting, Spencer. You were over the limit. Court cases, driving ban — maybe even prison. It would have meant an end to Greystone's interest. And as for Thelma, well . . . ' He leant back down. 'So you took it on your toes, as we say in the trade. And by the time Bob and I came back from Brussels, you had decided that the petrol was too expensive in Britain, and

171

had sold your car.'

If there was anything about Spencer's demeanour to confirm what Holt was saying, it was that it didn't change. It remained studiously, unnaturally, unchanged.

'Are you going to deny it?' Holt asked.

'I could,' said Spencer. 'It's pure conjecture.'

'It is on my part,' Holt said. 'But it wasn't conjecture on Allsopp's part, was it? I expect he took pretty pictures of the whole thing. Good photographer, wasn't he?'

Spencer, who never fought when he knew he was beaten, inclined his head a little. 'Are you going to tell Thelma?' he asked.

'Nothing to do with me,' said Holt. 'Is it?' He stood up straight again, and felt his back. Damn it, there was nothing wrong with it before she started massaging it. 'But I didn't cross you off,' he said. 'A man who was capable of driving away from that might well be capable of murder.'

Spencer removed a cigarette from the packet in front of him and tapped it on the table.

'All through the trial,' Holt said, 'I was told how I'd been having an affair with Alison. It had been going on for months. But I hadn't.'

Spencer frowned a little, and lit his cigarette, the flare from his lighter accentuating the gloom of the room.

'It's getting dark in here,' Holt said, going to the light switch. The lights flickered on, and the thunder rumbled again. 'Terrible weather,' he said to Cassie, who sat with her hand over her mouth, looking sick. She took her hand away, and Holt thought she might be going to say something, but she didn't.

'Why don't you get on with it?' Spencer said.

'Where was I? Oh, yes. Alison and her extra-marital affair.' His eyes went to Cassie again, but she looked away. 'It did seem that she involved herself with a lot of men,' he said. 'Why not you?'

'Maybe because I never met her,' Spencer said.

'Could have been. On the other hand, you might have been lying. You do see my predicament, don't you? Someone was lying.'

172

To the sound of Bryant's fingers tapping on the blotter, he toured the table, picking up his chair on the way, and sat between Spencer and Bryant. 'You were here that afternoon,' he said. 'You said you were taking photographs; you even said you didn't have a witness. I don't mind telling you, I thought that stuff about a photographic competition was eyewash.'

Spencer listened impassively, smoke rising from his cigarette, and hanging in the still, heavy air.

'But you did have a witness,' said Holt. 'Alison.'

Bryant's fingers stopped tapping.

'You were behind us at the station. She saw you there. And then, she happened to look out of the bedroom window, when she was on the phone to someone.'

Cassie shifted slightly, and Holt could feel Jan's eyes on him. He waited, but still Cassie said nothing. 'Alison saw you,' he said to Spencer. 'She saw you taking your industry and the country-side photograph of the power station.' He glanced at Bryant. 'She saw a man with a camera, and she thought he was your private eye,' he said, sitting back and folding his arms. 'That he'd followed her.' He paused. 'And that's when I crossed you off,' he said to Spencer. 'Because Alison didn't know you from Adam.'

Bryant was cleaning his glasses with intense concentration. Holt turned back to him. 'The question was,' he said, 'who was Alison's lover? It's what you wanted to know – that's why you spied on her.' He shuddered. 'Being watched,' he said. 'Without knowing. Even in prison you know you're being watched.'

'I don't think,' Bryant said, polishing the glass until it shone, 'that you are in a position to question my morality.'

'True,' said Holt. 'I needed no second invitation. But frankly,' he said. 'I was surprised to have been invited at all.'

Bryant put down the glasses.

'You really didn't know Alison, did you?' Holt said. 'You didn't try to know her. Once you'd got the ring on her finger, your future was assured. As long as you could hang on to her long enough. You might have had some doubt at the time, but you really believe it now, don't you? You really believe that Alison was sleeping around.'

'She told me she was,' Bryant replied.

173

'I don't think we need listen to any more of this,' Cartwright said. 'If he won't leave, we should.' He made to get up.

'Sit down, Charles,' Holt said. 'It would be very impolite to leave.'

Charles looked at Bryant, then at the others. 'We don't have to stay here and listen to this lunatic,' he shouted.

'Perhaps they want to,' Holt said. 'Perhaps they want to hear what I've got to say.'

'You were interested enough a moment ago,' Spencer said.

Cartwright sat down.

'Thank you,' said Holt. 'Yes, Bob, my behaviour left much to be desired. But at least I knew Alison well enough to know that she wasn't laying half the men in Greystone, whatever she said.'

'What was she doing then?' Bryant muttered.

Holt looked at Cassie.

'You were cock-a-hoop when Alison married you, weren't you, Bob?' he said, after a moment. 'Ralph Grey's only child, young and beautiful into the bargain. It was some bargain, wasn't it? And Ralph's blessing, even though you were divorced and almost old enough to be her father.' He sucked in his breath. 'But Ralph's a businessman, Bob. You should have known there would be a catch.'

Cassie wasn't looking at him. At anyone.

'She was seeing someone,' Holt said. 'Not the Brigade of Guards, just one person. But Allsopp did the dirty on you, Bob. You must have been his favourite client ever. He struck gold with you. He'd made enough in one week to pack his boring job in. Because he was blackmailing Alison instead of reporting to you.' He turned. 'Why are you letting me do this?' he shouted suddenly, at Cassie. 'Because you think I won't tell them? Well sod that, Cassie. Sod that!'

The eyes, except Jan's, all went to Cassie. Jan looked at him reproachfully. Well, he'd warned her. And he'd given Cassie plenty of chances to tell them herself. But she hadn't taken them.

Holt stood up and walked round, bending down between Jan and Cassie. 'That's what you said, wasn't it, Cassie?'

Cassie didn't speak.

'You were being blackmailed. Alison thought she'd paid him

off, but then that day — the day she died — she got that photograph of herself in the post. The one you didn't think worth explaining to the police, Bob,' he said, still looking at Cassie. 'And that afternoon, Alison went to see Allsopp; I've got it right, haven't I, Cassie?'

Cassie covered her face.

'Your secret is out,' Holt whispered melodramatically. 'Your secret, Cassie, not Alison's. Alison wanted to talk about it, and she rang you because she thought that you might object.'

Cassie looked at him, her eyes bright with the tears that she was holding back. 'I thought you'd had your pound of flesh,' she said.

Cartwright was looking away, and Bryant stared blankly into space. Spencer smoked, unperturbed.

'My pound of flesh,' mused Holt. 'You think that's what I'm after? Yes,' he said thoughtfully. 'Perhaps it is.' He fetched his chair, and placed it between Cassie and Charles. 'But I had to consider you, Cassie,' he said. 'You say you were at home, and that Alison rang you. But it's a bit like Wendy, isn't it? No one asked you to prove it.'

'I did prove it,' she said, wiping her eyes. 'I told you what she said.'

'But how do I know she rang you? How do I know that you were at home? You left work early; how do I know that you didn't just pop over to see Alison, and discover what she was doing? How do I know she didn't tell you about it after I'd gone?'

Cassie searched unsuccessfully for a tissue; Wendy gave her one of hers. Holt glanced at Jan, but she wasn't even looking at him now. She was covering Cassie's hand with hers, patting it gently.

'I was at home,' Cassie said, the words muffled by the handkerchief. 'I told you what she said.'

'You told me now. Sixteen years after the event. Once you knew all the facts. That's not proof, Cassie.'

She blew her nose. 'I would never have hurt Alison,' she said. 'Never. And you know that.'

Jan was truly angry with him now.

'Yes,' he said. 'I know. But knowing isn't proof, is it? So I

175

carried out a reconstruction. I knew *when* Alison saw Spencer. And so did you.'

He stood up as rain began to splash into the room, and went over to the window. 'That's when I crossed you off,' he said.

He closed the window. 'I think you loved Alison,' he said. 'And I think I was sacrificed because she loved you.'

He came back to the table. 'You were a puzzle, Charles,' he said, sitting down again, hooking one leg over the other. 'Why could you possibly have wanted to kill Alison?'

Cartwright looked back at him. 'I'm interested to hear,' he said.

'No reason. None that I could fathom.'

Thunder bumped round the sky.

'But you thought Bryant was paranoid – that was the word, wasn't it?'

Charles, permanently pink, looked down, and picked up his pen. He started to doodle while Holt spoke.

'Odd thing about psychology,' Holt said. 'It's the one branch of medicine that everyone thinks they understand. People who wouldn't dream of whipping out your appendix make judgements on your state of mind.' He turned back to Cartwright. 'He even accused you of making love – is that a nicer expression, Charles? – to his wife. And you saw your rosy future crumble away.'

The rain stopped, as though someone had turned it off, and bright sunlight slanted into the room, making the fluorescent lights redundant. Holt rose and switched them off. 'There's a rainbow,' he said. 'Come and look.'

No one was watching him now. Except Jan. Everyone else was staring at Charles, who was trying to behave as though they weren't.

'You had had your future snatched from you for something you hadn't done,' Holt continued. 'I know what that's like, Charles. That can make you want to kill.'

'You're mad,' Cartwright said, his eyes wide.

'There you go again,' said Holt, his voice scolding. 'And the worst of it was, you could have married Alison, if you'd moved faster. She'd have suited you, wouldn't she? You like beautiful

176

things, and she was beautiful. Like your paintings, and your music, and your sculptures.'

The fair lashes hid Cartwright's eyes, as he doodled on the pad in front of him.

'And now you were being falsely accused; none of the gravy and all of the blame. And you decided that Bryant had to go, didn't you?'

Charles drew a careful, complex rose on his pad.

'He's still trying to get rid of you, Bob,' Holt said.

Bryant frowned, and Cartwright's lips went into a thin, angry line.

'Oh, sorry,' said Holt. 'Wasn't I supposed to say?' He turned back to Bryant. 'Spencer and Wendy are in on it,' he said. 'I thought you might like to know.'

Wendy began to protest, but he talked her down.

'Back to the real world,' he said. 'You wanted rid of him then, didn't you, Charles? And when he got that call from Alison, you knew she had upset him somehow. It was a chance. A chance to take away something of his, to ruin his future. To get him suspected and accused, and you could sail into your rosy future again.'

Cartwright wasn't flushed any more. His eyes regarded Holt without emotion. 'Quite mad,' he said.

'Did Alison tell you someone was watching? And did you spend the next two weeks finding out about Allsopp? It wouldn't have been difficult; the police interviewed him. Easy enough to find him.'

Charles shook his head in disbelief.

'It was Bob that you set out to frame, but it had gone wrong, because the police had let him go. So I was the fall guy. How did you find out about me? Did Alison tell you?'

Cartwright still shook his head, a little sadly.

'Well?' said Holt. 'What do you think?'

'I think you need help,' said Cartwright slowly.

'But you could have done it.'

'No,' said Cartwright. 'I couldn't. I simply didn't have time.'

'Time. Oh, of course not. You saw Bryant just before seven, didn't you? You couldn't possibly have got there and back in that space of time. But then, we only have *your* word for that, don't we? Bryant doesn't know when the hell he saw you; you were giving *him* an alibi, after all. You say that you saw Spencer, too, but he doesn't seem to remember that.'

Spencer looked surprised, and shook his head.

'I didn't say he saw me!' Charles was losing his air of visiting social worker. 'I saw *him*, getting into the lift.'

'Where were you when Allsopp died?' Holt asked, then tapped himself on the head. 'Oh, of course,' he said. 'You were on a train.'

'Yes I was,' said Cartwright, at last looking hot under the collar. 'I was on a train from London.'

'On the train,' said Holt. 'Spencer thinks he was on that train too.' He turned to Spencer. 'Do you remember seeing Charles this time?' he asked.

Spencer shrugged.

'You remember,' Cartwright said, a touch desperately. 'We met in the buffet car, just before the train got here.'

'Oh, yes,' Spencer said. 'I think I remember now.'

'That train had to stop right beside where Allsopp lived,' said Holt, conversationally. 'For about a minute or so, because of that station extension here.'

Charles had recovered his composure. 'I see,' he said. 'So I jumped off the train, murdered Allsopp, and got back on?' He said each word carefully, as though he were talking to a very small child. A very small child with a meat cleaver.

'No,' said Holt seriously. 'That would have been impossible. Allsopp was dead before the train got there. No,' he said, straddling the chair again. 'You were on the train, and you stayed on it. You were doing my job; I couldn't do it because I had an appointment with Allsopp. So you couldn't possibly have got to Allsopp before I did. And that,' he said, looking round at his audience, 'is when I crossed Charles off.'

It was Charles who broke the silence that followed.

'I told you,' he said. 'I told you when he came here that this was what he was going to do.'

'Most of it for my benefit,' Cassie said, her voice shaking. 'All of it. Some sort of sick revenge for what Alison did. You had to punish me.'

'Revenge,' Holt said, nodding. 'Yes. That must be it. I must have done it after all. That's why they locked me up for so long.'

'He's mad,' Cartwright said.

'No, he's not.' Cassie stood up. 'He knows exactly what he's doing.'

'Do I?' said Holt. 'You see, I can't remember killing anyone. Bob thinks I must get blackouts – that's probably the answer.' He smiled at Cassie. 'Why don't you sit down?' he said.

'I'm not afraid of — '

'Sit down, Cassie!' Cartwright said.

She sat down. 'He's playing with us,' she said. 'I know.'

'It just seemed to me,' Holt said slowly, 'that I'd remember if I'd beaten Alison unconscious and strangled her. Allsopp . . . well, that might slip my mind. I mean, who needed him? But Alison? I think that would have made an impression on me. Still,' he said, standing up and taking the chair back to the wall. 'Sixteen years is a long time. Things do get a bit hazy.'

'Look, Bill, I think you should — ' Spencer began.

'But then,' Holt said, talking through him, 'I realised where I had been going wrong.'

Spencer raised an eyebrow, and looked round at the others with a slight shrug, as Holt walked back to the table, and crouched down between Jan and Cassie.

'You see, Cassie,' he said, but Cassie turned her head away. Holt paused, then continued to talk to her anyway. 'Alison didn't die because of what she did to me,' he said. 'She didn't die because of who she was, or what she was, or because she phoned Bob. I'd been looking for someone who wanted Alison dead,' he said. 'But though, God knows, she caused a lot of trouble for a lot of people, the fact is that no one wanted Alison dead.'

Cassie moved her head slightly, and he could see her face, her eyes, a flicker of interest in them. 'Then why was she killed?' she asked.

'Because I didn't order a taxi,' Holt said, standing up. 'We'd all got it the wrong way round. Allsopp didn't die because he knew too much about Alison's murder. Alison knew too much about his.'

179

Nineteen

'After I'd crossed everyone off,' said Holt, 'I was left with a question.' He walked up to Spencer. 'Why did Alison think you were following her?' he asked.

'I thought you'd explained to us why,' said Spencer.

'No. Alison left Greystone to meet me at the station. She and I were the only two people in the world who knew that was where she was going. And when she got there, she saw you. In the station. And you saw her. You mentioned that she kissed me, remember? We were still in the station when she kissed me.'

He went to the window, and looked out at the quiet road. 'So how could she have thought that you had followed her there?' he asked. 'You were obviously there before she was.'

'I don't know,' said Spencer, as though Holt were asking a riddle. 'How could she have thought that I was following her?'

'Because she had seen you earlier,' said Holt. 'She said so. "Ask whoever's been following me all day" — those were her words, weren't they, Bob? We both remember exactly what she said.'

Bryant nodded.

'You did follow her,' Holt said. 'You went to where you could see the house, and that's when you thought up your phoney competition.' He reached into his jacket pocket, and took out the photographs. Alison, Jan. The power station. Miles away. He threw it on the table. 'Exhibit A,' he said. 'That's the view you get of the power station. You should have used a telephoto lens; Allsopp could have told you that.'

'So I didn't win,' said Spencer. 'I've improved.'

Holt was aware of the general air of discomfort, of disbelief. But Cassie was listening.

'And then Alison did her strip-tease for you,' he said. Poor unhappy Alison. Tears for Alison pricked his eyes at last. He blinked them away. 'And when I left, you knew she was alone. So you went down, let yourself in, and killed her.'

'Look, Bill,' Cartwright said. 'Perhaps . . . ' He paused. 'All right,' he said. 'Perhaps you didn't kill them. But you can't just accuse people. Perhaps you should see someone.'

'You're at it again, Charles,' Holt said.

Cartwright spoke gently, carefully. 'What reason would Jeff have for doing something like that?' he asked. 'He didn't even know Alison.'

'No, he didn't. He had no idea who she was. It didn't matter who she was.' He turned away, and wiped a tear that had escaped the blink. 'She didn't even know why it was happening to her,' he said, and there was silence. Holt didn't turn round. He couldn't.

'I think Charles is right,' said Spencer. 'I think you need help.'

Holt turned then. 'I got help,' he said, walking over to Jan. 'That's why you're not dead, Spencer.' He put his hands on Jan's shoulders, and could feel the tension. He bent down. 'Relax,' he whispered in her ear, and she smiled a little.

'Allsopp was blackmailing you,' he said to Spencer. 'But you were a hustler, Jeff. A con man. You didn't have a brass farthing. You'd bought your computer business on the strength of a non-existent link-up with Greystone. Whose signature did you forge? Bryant's? Ralph Grey's? No matter. What mattered was that you didn't have any money to pay Allsopp off; and if you didn't pay him off, you'd lose what you did have. A rich widow, and your liberty. Because you would have been done for fraud on top of everything else.'

He pulled the chair back out from the wall, as Cartwright's face lost its disbelief, and began to look interested. He sat beside Jan, who held his hand tightly.

'Allsopp had to go,' he said.

'I think Cartwright had a point earlier on,' Spencer said. 'We really don't have to sit and listen to this.'

Cartwright looked up from his pad, on which he had doodled dozens of roses, complete with thorns. He laid down his pen and regarded Spencer. 'This sudden support for my opinion is very gratifying,' he said, 'but I'd like to hear what Bill has to say.'

Bryant stared at Cartwright, then at Spencer.

'Well, Mr Chairman?' asked Holt. 'Show of hands, do you think?'

Bryant looked helplessly round, then back to Holt. 'Just get on with it,' he snapped.

'You sold your car, and started taking the train on your trips here,' said Holt. 'The train having to stop where it did gave you the idea.'

'Oh,' laughed Spencer. 'I'm Superman, now. I can get off a train, sprint quarter of a mile, murder someone, do the return journey and get back on the train in sixty seconds.'

'No.' Holt shook his head. 'There's another way. You get the morning train instead. You get off at the station before, walk to the old station, and wait until it's time. Kill Allsopp, then stroll back through the woods, and *wait* for the bloody afternoon train!'

Wendy looked thoughtful, and glanced at Charles, who sat back a little, considering Spencer.

'That's why you didn't see him until you were practically here, Charles. Because he wasn't on the train until you were practically here.'

He turned back to Spencer. 'But you couldn't do it cold,' he said. 'You had to know whether or not you would have enough time, and whether or not you *could* get on the train without anyone noticing. That bit was easy, I expect. With an express train coming the other way, no one would hear. Smack between stations, no one would be waiting at the doors. But you had to test it; never do anything at random. And it worked. That part worked.'

Bryant was sitting forward, his reading glasses, polished to a twinkling brightness, abandoned.

'In fact, you thought it had all worked. Yes, you'd met a girl near Allsopp's caravan, but that didn't matter. You didn't know her and she didn't know you. It didn't matter until you saw her again. Meeting me.'

Spencer was turning the ring round and round his finger as he listened, an expression of amused incomprehension carefully arranged on his face.

'All Alison saw was the man who had seen her at Allsopp's. And now he was behind her going home. And then he was outside her house with a camera. She didn't stop to work out the logistics.'

Cassie took another tissue.

'But you saw danger. Because I'd seen you on the train. A train you couldn't, logically, have *been* on. If Alison and I ever discussed the matter, your alibi was blown.'

There was no movement from Spencer, save the twisting of the ring.

'Of course, there was no likelihood of our discussing it, not then. But once Allsopp was dead . . . ' Holt stopped for a moment. 'And he had to die, or you would be ruined. You had no idea who Alison was. She could have been Allsopp's wife, his sister; you didn't know how deep her interest would be in his death. All that mattered was that she knew Allsopp, and I knew you, and the circle had to be broken.'

Spencer lit a cigarette.

'So you broke it. Then you drove into town, and saw Ralph's car still here. So you went up to establish an alibi. And then . . . then the police were looking for me, so you refined your plan for Allsopp. You'd got a meeting with him. So you sent me that letter, copying Allsopp's signature this time. If I took the bait, you were home free. If I didn't, you were no worse off. You still had your alibi.'

Spencer released smoke with an audible sigh.

'And of course I took the bait; I couldn't have Allsopp turning up on my doorstep.' Holt sat back. 'Never do anything at random,' he said. 'You'd had to kill Alison without much forethought, but you planned this one, all right. You thought of everything, didn't you? Right down to leaving the envelope unsealed.'

'Excuse me?' Spencer said, the first time he had spoken.

Holt addressed the assembly. 'Spencer knew what could be traced, and what couldn't,' he said. 'Typewritten letters can be traced, so he made Allsopp a posthumous present of a typewriter. The flaps on envelopes can give you away; saliva, and even how they've been licked. True, Spencer?'

'If you say so,' said Spencer, sitting back in an attitude of smiling comfort.

'You couldn't trust your fists with Allsopp,' Holt said. 'He was much taller than you, and a man might put up more of a fight. So you used an iron bar. And I got his blood on my sleeve — that must have made you chuckle, Spencer.'

There was silence for a moment, then Spencer sat up, looking vaguely surprised. 'Sorry,' he said. 'Are you waiting for me to say something?'

Holt felt Jan squeeze his hand. 'Excuse me,' she murmured, as she got up. 'I'll wait in the car.'

Everyone watched her as she crossed the room, and went out.

'You're losing your audience, Bill,' said Spencer. 'Don't you think you should go after her?'

'No,' said Holt. 'What Jan does is her business.'

'Speaking of business,' said Spencer, sitting round to face the table. 'If the floor-show's over, we've got work to do.'

'There was what my barrister called conflicting evidence,' Holt went on. 'Fingerprints that couldn't be identified.'

Spencer smiled. 'Is this where I'm supposed to say that I didn't leave any fingerprints?'

'I'm sure you did,' said Holt. 'You hadn't planned killing Alison. It was the middle of summer — a beautiful day, I seem to recall. You wouldn't be wearing gloves.'

'No, I shouldn't think I was,' smiled Spencer.

'But no one asked for your fingerprints,' Holt said, standing up. 'And no one's going to.'

He put his chair and Jan's neatly against the wall. 'I want to leave everything as I found it,' he said. 'I'm sorry about the intrusion, Mr Chairman, but I thought you all ought to know as much as I do.' He smiled coldly. 'He'd have to murder us all, and I think people might start to suspect something. They say there's safety in numbers. Let's hope they're right.'

Jan was waiting for him in the car. He slumped, exhausted, frustrated, and angry. Angry because there was nothing anyone could do and that smiling bastard would just walk away from it all.

184

'Well?' he said, not lifting his head.

'You were cruel to Cassie,' she said.

'I said you wouldn't like it. I wanted to be cruel.'

She didn't say anything, and he looked up. 'Is that it? End of lecture?'

'Yes.' She stroked the back of his neck.

He had thought he would feel better. Maybe he really had hoped that Spencer would break down and confess, or slip up and give himself away. Chance would be a fine thing.

'They listened,' Jan said.

'I know. But they can't do anything. Even if they believed me. And he's probably convincing them right now that I'm round the bend.'

Jan smiled at him. 'The fat lady hasn't sung yet,' she said, opening the briefcase, and taking out the cassette player. 'Listen to her.'

Ralph's gruff voice spoke.

'. . . *said he was using a portable typewriter now, but that soon it would be a portable . . .*'

Jan switched it off.

Holt frowned a little, not sure what it meant. So, Spencer had had a portable typewriter. So had lots of people. He sighed. 'I don't suppose he was obliging enough to give the make and serial number, was he?' he said, with the closest he could get to a smile.

'Probably not,' said Jan. 'But Ralph was obliging enough to keep the letter.'

She packed away the cassette player, snapping shut the briefcase. 'It's a wonderful thing, old technology,' she said. 'You can tell if two letters have been typed on the same machine.'

Holt couldn't speak.

'You can't any more, of course,' she carried on, smiling at him. 'Not now that it's all daisy wheels and dot matrix —'

'But that's evidence!' he shouted, finding his voice. 'Real, honest-to-God *evidence*.' And he kissed her, a winger kissing a striker. 'When did you realise?' he demanded.

'In there. When you said about his posthumous gift to Allsopp. I came down to find the bit on the tape.'

'Evidence,' he said again. 'Real evidence. *New* evidence, not

185

available to the jury.'

'Bill,' she said. 'You know it could take months, years, even. They don't like admitting mistakes. And even if you do get a pardon — and you shouldn't really count on that — it doesn't mean that Spencer will — '

He was kissing her again, in mid-flow, with rather more finesse than before.

'I've got something for you,' he said, reaching into his jacket pocket. 'Not chocolates,' he added hastily.

She took the envelope he handed her. 'What is it?' she asked.

'The nearest I could get to a magic train.'

He watched her as she opened the envelope and drew out the tickets.

'The Orient Express,' she said. 'Oh, Bill, how *lovely!*'

He smiled. 'For you and the companion of your choice,' he said. 'That seems to be me, for some reason.'

'It's you.' She was reading the tickets. 'It's wonderful,' she said, then looked at him. 'Except . . . '

'What?' he asked, dismayed.

'The Orient Express?' she said.

They laughed. And for a moment, it seemed just possible that one day he would lose the cold grey feeling inside.

One day.